Rainbear!!!!!!!!!

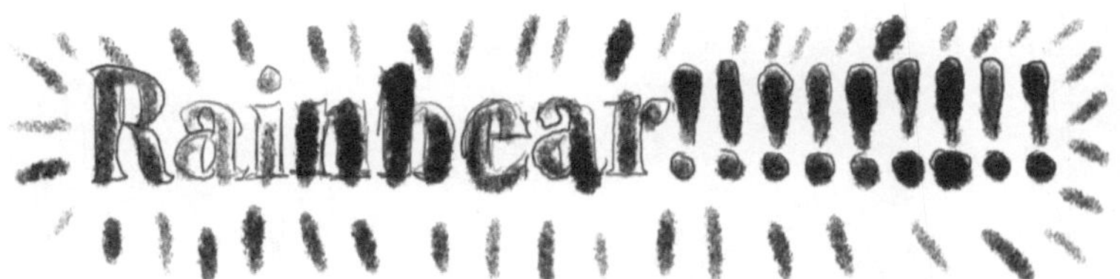

by

Never Angeline North

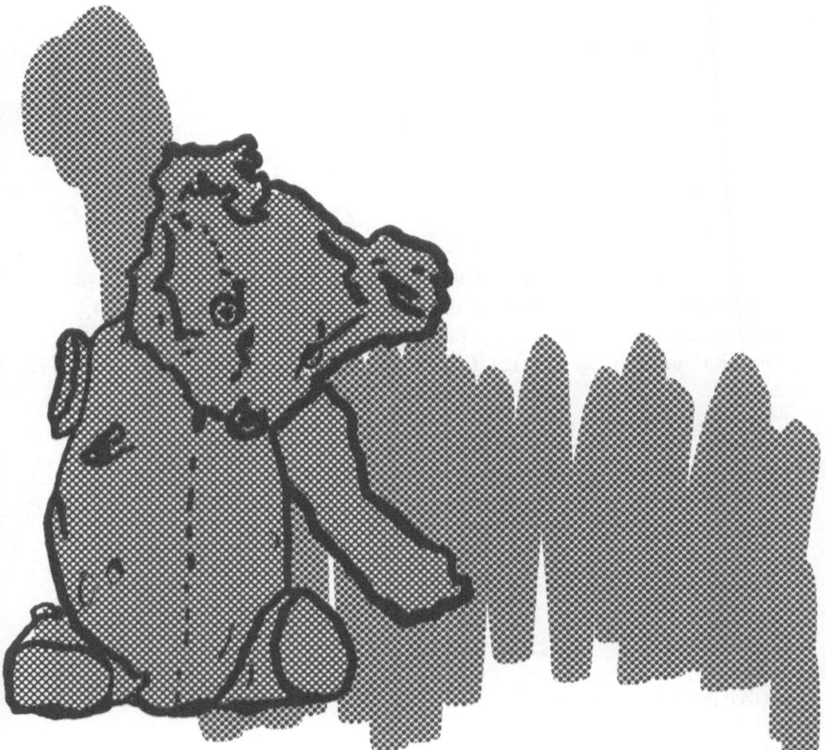

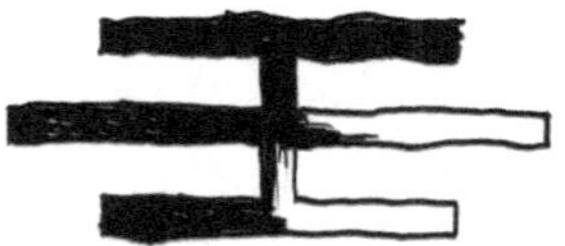

Apocalypse Party

Design by Mike Corrao and Never Angeline Nørth
Cover Design by Never Angeline Nørth
Cover Art by Sharada Tolton

Paperback: 978-1-954899-08-7

Printed in the United States of America

FIRST AMERICAN EDITION

9 8 7 6 5 4 3 2 1

Rainbear.........!!!!!!!

by

Never Angeline North

In memory of Kristie Shoemaker: slug-admirer & fellow member
of the beautiful creatures club.

BINAH

Chapter One

Forget everything you've been taught. Start by dreaming.

- graffiti from the May 1968 Paris protests

I like to fall asleep to ocean sounds played from my phone. I close my eyes and imagine myself in a beach house. Fantasize until the images slip into dream.

The salt smell.

A body washes ashore covered in tattoos that tell me what will happen. All over its skin are forty, maybe fifty large-ish outline portraits of the same man with different facial expressions. They are done in a number of different colors. The magic is all in the eyes. The eyes of each little tattooed portrait tell me so many things. Interpreting these images isn't interpretive, like reading a fortune. It's more like a map, like somebody's plans. Like God had been writing notes for her own use, and they showed up in the form of facial expressions, delicately tattooed in portraits across the skin of a lifeless corpse washed up on the beach. My beach.

The beach house has a worn porch that faces the water and I can hear the sounds of dolphins playing from my kitchen window while I cook. I keep the windows open and a breeze blows through the house, making the linen curtains dance. I decide these curtains are coral, and that I have an old basset hound who I need to bathe frequently in order to keep the sand from getting up into his paws and getting infected. I never mind doing this, in the dream, and the dog likes the warm water of the tub.

God's map contains a delightful series of nothing-muches, small delights and surprises to fill my life with joy. It is primarily oriented around me and my immediate environs. There is an excellent bit about my dog's relationship with a cloud that will be coming up in the next ten years, and so I make plans to make sure I am outside to watch it happen.

Nobody ever comes to ask about the body. It isn't that kind of fantasy.

•°•

When I wake up from my dream, I am at the coffee shop again. The barista has turned off my ocean sounds and so I look up and give him a scowl. He mewls at me. They hate me at this coffee shop, but I love them. Even when they turn off my ocean sounds while I am sleeping, I love them. My love keeps this coffee shop open. People come to me here, in this coffee shop, for my love, which I give to them.

Sometimes they also buy coffee, either as an offering to me in exchange for my love (which is ill-advised because I do not drink coffee) or to drink themselves while I love them. I will love them no matter who they are. No matter how tall or bearfaced. No matter if they have coffee breath or anything.

Today I had a man come in and show me his hands. He showed me all the parts of his hands, the insides of his fingers and the backs and middles. I watched him make shapes with them: a heart, a flying bird, both the North American and UK "fuck you" gestures, two feet with extremely long toes where his arms are like the legs, a rock, church/steeple, etc.. I told him I loved him, which I did. I don't love him now but he isn't here now, and if he was here, I would love him once more. I have become extremely good at loving the people who sit in the chair across from me. I have loved groups of up to 15-20 people at a time. 34 once. They barely fit in my coffee shop.

They were a tourist group from Prince Edward Island. I loved them so much. I don't any longer, but in the moment I did so very much. I don't think I would have any time to do anything if I continued to love everyone after they left.

I press my fingers to my temples and turn on my ocean sounds again, but to no avail. A woman comes from the bathroom and I ask her if she is here to be loved. "No," she says. "I am here to leave."

At this point, the barista cuts in. He jumps over the coffee counter and flashes a badge on his jacket. It is shiny, brass, and shield-shaped and says "badge" on it in all caps. BADGE. "Which outside did you come in from?" he asks.

"She came from the bathroom," I toss in, hoping to help. The barista mewls at me again.

"That outside," the barista points to a row of doors on one side of the coffee shop, "is different from this outside," he points to the row of doors on the other side, "and bad things could happen if we start allowing people from one outside into the other outside. So what outside did you come in from?"

The woman seems to ponder his question. She opens her mouth and a single mother comes out. The barista holds up a finger to the woman and shows his BADGE badge to the single mother. The single mother points to the set of doors on the left side of the room, so the barista pulls a key on an extendable keychain attached to his belt and unlocks one of the doors on the left side of the room. The single mother shuffles out, turns into a moth and flies away, glowing with her own internal light. The barista locks the door again and returns to the woman.

"So which is it?" says the barista.

"What happens if I get it wrong?" says the woman.

"Do you plan to get it wrong?" The barista says, eyeing her suspiciously.

"The left side?" She floats the words into the air like she is worried she may never get them back.

"My left or your left?" the barista asks, still eyeing her.

"Her left." She points to me. I look to my left and realize she means the bathroom. The only thing to my left is the bathroom. The woman turns and runs into the bathroom. The barista stands still for a while, still eyeing, but now he is eyeing the bathroom door suspiciously and begins to feel a little bit silly. He looks at me and mewls, then hops the counter to resume his post as barista. I am silently laughing, but it is stress laughter. All my laughter is stress laughter. I think about how the word "laughter" looks like "daughter" but doesn't sound like it. I imagine pronouncing them in reverse. "Dafter." "Lotter."

After some time passes the door to the bathroom opens a crack and the woman peeks out.

"Psst," she says to me.

"Pssssst," I say back.

"Could you love me now?"

I nod and get up and enter the bathroom. When I enter the bathroom, I take her hands and I have sex with them. For some people, love and sex are the same thing. For other people, they are the opposite. Once I have had sex with her hands, I wash them gently in the sink. "Thank you," she whispers to me, even though we are all alone.

"For what?" I ask, even though I know.

"For helping."

"I didn't help, though. I made you feel better about being unhelpable. That's what love is. It doesn't solve anything. It is the opposite of solving, in that it is capable of allowing us to live while having no solutions. It makes the terrible bearable. Just enough for us to stay in it."

"I don't believe that," she tells me. "And I don't think you do either." At that, I eye her suspiciously, but she has caught on now, and begins eyeing me suspiciously right back. I mewl at her and leave the bathroom. When I re-enter the coffee shop, the sprinkler system is on, everything is drenched and the barista is standing behind the counter, his wet hair plastered to his head. I contemplate returning to my chair, but instead I come up to the counter. I open my mouth wide, and he leans forward and mewls deeply inside. I feel it echo through my whole being. He puts up wallpaper inside my mouth and installs a fireplace there. He lays brick that creates a chimney emerging from my right cheek. He starts the fire, I blow it out. He starts the fire, I blow it out. I push him away. I close the flu. "Excuse you," I say to him. He grins at me like a maniac. I return to my chair in a huff. "Excuse you," I mumble to myself.

•º•

Tonight I am sleeping under the table in my coffee shop, curled like an animal. The barista sleeps spread out on the shop counter with his head on the register like a pillow. I used to tease him for the marks it left on his face when he woke up. But teasing is something you do as a type of play. I used to do a lot of things I don't do now. I used to sleep on that counter next to him.

I turn on the sounds of the ocean from my phone, plugged into an outlet near my head. Tonight it is more difficult to get into my beach house because of the chimney in my face. It is my fantasy, and so I try to take it apart, brick by brick, but the bricks keep flying back into place like magnets.

When I finally begin to drift off, I think briefly about the woman in the bathroom. I imagine her sleeping next to me, and as the ocean sounds begin to mix with my thoughts, I imagine her inside my beach house with me. "Sweet angel," I call her. "Sweet angel, will you make the coffee today? I did it yesterday."

I do not actually remember whether or not I made the coffee

yesterday, because while in the world of this dream we have lived together for a long time, I do not possess a specific detailed memory of the entire time. I wonder briefly if it is manipulative for me to tell her I did it yesterday. Then I wonder if it is the kind of manipulative that is cute and playful and transparent or the kind that eats away at a person. That thought is followed up by a sense of revulsion at myself for having the idea that any manipulation at all could be cute, playful or clearly transparent. I can't tell whether or not I am judging myself too harshly. I table the thought for later and realize she is already making the coffee. I go to her.

The dolphins make their sounds which, as ever, float in on the breeze gently fluttering our coral-toned linen curtains. I take her in my arms. I tell her that the interpretive notes on God's tattooed man told me that "we were meant to always be together my sweet angel," which in this dream I am deciding is true. She rolls her eyes at me and returns to our coffee. When she leans over, I notice her hair falls to one side, revealing an eminently nibbleable ear. She glances up at me, blows a kiss in my direction, and follows it with a wink, which I return.

On the west side of the house is a pool of cum, from the middle of which emerges a very large penis, frequently spurting cum. Right now it is soft, flopped right over in its own little pool, so I take a break from my flirtations and step outside to cuddle it a little. It doesn't take long to get it fully stiff (I wouldn't call it hard, because the skin is so soft!) and so I fuck it some, and then go into the ocean to wash the cum from my hair and skin and asshole. Salt water is very good for the skin and hair. As is cum. When sweet angel calls my name, I return to her, wet and salty.

After coffee, we go for a walk on the beach with the dog. When we get to the edge, where beach meets forest, she presses me against the tree, flips her hair to one side and offers me her ear to nibble, which I do. Giggles emit from both parties.

The next morning, I awake to the barista getting stabbed and my face still contains a chimney. He gets stabbed around once a week, by a man and a woman who come in and stab him for a few hours without saying much. He avoids eye contact with me while this happens, and I am deeply thankful. This stabbing thing has been going on for years. I used to comfort him, love him whenever he was stabbed, but there was a point where I had to stop. I like to think of myself as a kind woman, and I feel terrible for how frequently he is stabbed, but what am I supposed to do? Love him forever just because I feel bad and we're in the same room? That would only be fair if I was able to love everyone who is being stabbed, no matter their distance from me. And that I cannot do. Too much research! The cafe would close. What table would I sleep under then?

I think of my dream, of my sweet angel. I go to the bathroom door and open it. The door, in turn, opens me back. We both open widely, to flowers.

"I'm seeing someone," I tell the door. "I see so many people," I tell it.

"I can't see you," says the door. "I'm a door," it says.

I cry some and return to my seat. A man sits opposite me with a bee in each nostril. "I love you," I tell him. "I love you so deeply," I say. He cries and I cry with him.

"I can't love you back," he tells me.

"That's okay," I take his hand.

"I'm committed to someone," he says, gesturing to a choir that is currently ordering one Italian soda for each of its mouths.

"I understand," I tell him. "I still love you," I say.

At this point, he leans over and whispers in my ear, "My choir wouldn't understand if they knew you loved me. Even if they knew absolutely without a doubt that I don't love you back, they wouldn't understand." At this point, one of his bees stings my cheek.

I put my mouth to his ear and do some whispering of my own. "Fuck your choir." I let the words seep into his ear. "And fuck you." I pause and sit back in my chair. "I don't love you anymore," I say at full volume, vaguely hoping the choir overhears.

The man cries. I relax, because my job here is done. Unloving someone is incredibly important. As important as loving them. He made it easier by stinging me with his nose bee. Nothing could make me love him after that. Until he returns, of course.

More clients filter in and I love them each. I cry some. This is the first job I have had where crying helps. The other jobs I had discouraged crying at work. I would always spitefully cry at my bosses when they reminded me of this. I think about the concept of crying for awhile. How strange. How animal.

"I'm such a leaflet," I say to a client later, who pins me to a bulletin board and reads me before deciding he will not be able to attend after all.

"My daughter," he says apologetically while nodding his head towards his daughter, who cries as she works with tools to weave her hair into the side of his coat. "She has ballet."

I imagine her doing a whirling pirouette, her tears spiraling out around her, her hair loose and free. It is beautiful. "Don't worry about it," I want to say, but can't. I'm such a leaflet.

I let out a sigh, which blows me off the board and into a little loop-de-loop. I land in the trash. The man thanks me and leaves. The air in the coffee shop is strong today. It is a beautiful, strong air day.

• ○ •

The beach is perfect. The sea is orange, the sand is white and the sky is not full of knives. I hold my sweet angel and we sit on a blanket and watch the waves while our dog plays around us. I touch her hands. I kiss them. Our life together here is everything I could have wanted. I'm not thinking about manipulations anymore, subtle or otherwise. I kiss her hair and I feel like for the first time in my life I am not hiding anything at all.

"This is a dream," I say to her.

"God, I know," she says.

"No," I say, "I mean this is an actual dream. I am dreaming this."

"No, I know," she says. "I was calling you God."

"Why?" I ask her.

"That's what you are here," she tells me. "You are my God. The God of your dream. And I am part of that dream. I am your dream girl." She lays her head on my lap as our dog bites the waves rolling in.

I think about this as I stroke the small hairs on the back of her neck.

"Can I ask you something?"

"God, you can ask me anything."

"First, it is a little strange to be called God. I think I would not like to be called God anymore."

"Done. And second?"

"I have a confession."

"Confess, my love."

"I have always wanted to have a child."

Sweet angel sits up and looks at me seriously. She studies my face. She takes her hands and gently strokes both sides of my face with the backs of her knuckles.

"You will have a child. We will have a child. We will call it our child," she tells me.

I look into her eyes. "Really? In this place?"

"Yes. In this place. Our dream home. Our perfect child," she smiles at me.

I smile back.

The sky has no knives for us today, and our dog runs back to us excitedly, somehow younger than he used to be.

•°•

My chimney hurts all day at work. It feels like someone lit the fire in my mouth's fireplace while I was sleeping. Smoke pours from my face and the wallpaper crinkles as I speak, but I have no time for pain or frustration. A child. Our child. I don't use the bathroom all day. Instead, I take turns peeing out the doors. Pee is allowed to go out either door, but people are not. People can only go out one door. I can see the barista fingering his BADGE badge when I open them to pee. I can't tell if he really thinks I would leave or if he just wants an excuse to watch me pee. I have no idea if my sweet angel is in the bathroom still. I don't know when she would have gotten out. I almost don't care. I feel like I got what I needed from her, which feels like a cruel thing to say. But she can't hear my thoughts to be hurt by this. Finding her again here, in this broken place, would be too sad.

The barista looks at me like I am a crime, and my pee turns into potatoes as it crosses the door's threshold. "Here I am no one's God and no one's dream girl," I say out loud, as my potatoes thud, one by one, onto the forbidden topsoil.

CHAPTER TWO

When the Holy One
Blessed be She
Blessed be He
Blessed be It
Blessed be They
(for so our text tells us by giving us 'Elohim'-a plural)
awoke on the sixth day and got ready to work
all the angels gathered around
Her
Him
It
Them
and those angels
seeing what was going to unfold that good day
all said
concerning the creation of the first human being
"O Creator of all that is
do not do this. Do not
[...]

- Andrew Ramer, Fragments of the Brooklyn Talmud

"This is how we make a baby."

The dolphins are loud today as we sit out on the beach. Their calls are high and shrill. I calm myself down and remember that this is my dream. Here I am God. Not that I want to be God, but if that is true, which Sweet Angel seems to think it is, then how can I have anxiety? I can't, so I pull it into a hard ball in my body and imagine it floating off. Almost immediately it comes back like the bricks in my face's chimney when I tried to dream them apart. I touch my face. No chimney. I exhale.

"Take my hand," Sweet Angel holds out her hand.

"Yes. A baby!" I think of tiny feet and fingers looking for something to grasp. I smile involuntarily. I take her hand.

"Put my hand in your mouth," she says. I do.

"Good. Now I can tell you what to do, but you have to be the one who does it. I have no powers here. You are the one with the power."

"Rgrathrrth," I say. My drool trickles down her palm.

"Now take your other hand and put it in my pants." I do this. Her genitals are soft. I briefly wonder, since I am God, if I could make them hard. I feel her genitals begin to grow beneath my touch. It is possible that would have happened anyway, though, so I don't give this much credence.

"Good. I mean, that part isn't necessary, but you wanted to do it anyway, and it's fun."

"Mfrayrf," I slobber. The corners of my mouth widen as I grin back at her over her knuckles. I hold onto her bits firm and gentle, like I am holding an injured bird I don't want to escape.

"What we want here is total selfhood. Close your eyes. Now close them a second time without opening them first. Make them close twice. Fully. Okay, now think of the letters of your name. Picture them floating in space. Focus hard on their edges, their corners, their round parts. Don't think about how it sounds, or what it means, or who it represents. Just picture it. Focus as hard as you can on this picture. Feel yourself fall away. Feel the space get wider. Look at those letters. Let them stop being letters. Let them be shapes. Lose your language."

"Lulthf."

"You have no body. You have no mind. You are nothing to speak of. Nothing to see. You simply exist. Now stop existing. Dissolve the self. Dissolve the 'I'. There is no 'I'. No 'me.' You no longer understand my words. I am not transmitting them as words. Nothing exists. Not even me."

Sweet Angel stops speaking. Everything is quiet for what feels like a very long time.

A dolphin makes a particularly loud "E E E E EE" sound and I jolt back to reality. I open my eyes. Sweet Angel is no longer in front of me. I begin to panic, then I realize I can still feel soft skin in my hand. I still feel my hand in my mouth. I look at my hand. Inside there is the smallest infant I have ever seen. It is curled up in my palm, sucking its thumb. It is perfect. I use my other hand to remove the thing from my mouth. It is a hand. It is attached to nothing. There is no wrist.

I go back into the beach house and clean the sand from myself and everything. I take the baby and sit with it in bed. I kiss it but it does not awake. It is the softest thing I have ever felt. This is not an exaggeration. It is supernaturally soft. I cry a little. I make a little pool of blankets and set the baby in the middle of it so it will be warm and safe. I leave the room to find something to make a better bed. I find half of a large plastic egg filled with clean, loose silk. It is exactly the thing I imagined I would like to find. I realize I am still holding the hand. I look hard at it. There are tattoos along the back of it that I hadn't noticed. Overlapping squares. I do not know what they mean. This was not in God's notes. I put the hand inside the front of my underwear. It doesn't feel sexual. I am a mother.

•º•

I have no time to love anybody in this horrible coffee shop today. Immediately upon waking, a table fell on me. This is why I usually try to go to sleep under a table, so things don't fall on me, but this time it was the table I was asleep under that fell on me. My chimney is a pure tower of pain. I think it has developed nerve endings, and now it is like pushing on a giant infected tooth when I touch it. It occludes my vision. The fire in it got too warm overnight, so I drink water to put out the fire and choke on a piece of sloughed-off wallpaper. I mewl loud and long at the barista anytime I catch his line of sight coming even remotely close to me. "What the fuck, guy," I say to him. I do not know why I say this. My chair is directly in front of where his eyes would naturally rest while standing at the register and so my prickly nature forces him to spend a lot of time looking down at the counter or up at the ceiling.

A woman comes in and sits at my table for me to love her and when she puts her bag on the table it collapses again. I am about to tell her I love her but it comes out "I would love for you to eat my ass." I say it in a loud mean voice and not a sexual or love voice. The woman gets so flustered she turns to go out the opposite door she came in from and the barista throws a french press at her head. It misses and shatters all over the floor. My pant leg is all soaked and I keep finding bits of broken glass and coffee grounds in my left sock. Instead of fixing my table, I lay down on it and mewl at anyone who comes close to me. I don't love anyone all day. An orange cloud forms above me and rains tomato juice all over my body before dissipating. A blue cloud comes and rains gin and vermouth. My body lets off tiny bursts of steam when each drop hits me. Tssss. Tsss. Tssss. I roll onto my knees and lick from a boozy puddle like a little kitten.

Later, I army crawl into the bathroom to look for the woman who both is and isn't Sweet Angel. A corner of the sink has been gnawed on, the paper towel dispenser has been disassembled, and the linoleum is peeled up in the corner stall. It looks like she tunneled out. I plop myself down on the floor in the stall and gaze into the hole she left. "I love you," I yell into it. I yell, "Just kidding!" and then "Ok, no, I do!" I build a small city with my feelings and tear it down again. I push the ruins into the hole and spit on them. I mewl at myself and bang my shoulder and elbows against the wall. It hurts, but I'm okay. Just sad.

When I open the door back to the coffee shop, it tells me I am alive and I say "Yeah so what, bitch. Suck it." The barista has carved the word "REBAR" on my floor table. He acts busy cleaning out the espresso maker but I know he did it. We are the only ones in the room. I use a fork and alter it so it says A RARE BARE. I try to draw a tiny baby above it, but it doesn't turn out well, so I scratch it out and draw a dragon eating the barista. The dragon has a giant dick and is also farting, which I draw as a little poofy cloud with the word "FART" next to it. It takes up most of the table. I touch my chimney. The soreness has mostly faded, but it is still a little tender. I hear the barista mewling at me from across the room but I don't look up. I have nothing to say to him. I have everything I need. I have a baby. My tiny perfect little baby. In spite of myself, I smile.

•º•

That night, after the coffee shop closes, the barista puts his hand in mine and asks me if I want to sleep next to him on the counter, since my table is broken. I actually think about it, briefly, while looking at his stab wounds. They seem to be getting some kind of infection, and there is pus seeping from one on his thigh where his pants have ripped. I shake my head no and then spend the whole night building a yurt from plastic utensils. It has a futon made out of forks, which I cover with sewn-together napkins. I put a sign on the door that says NO BADGES ALLOWED.

I spend all morning on my fork futon vaping and blowing fake smoke rings out of my face-chimney. A man in a sailor suit comes in holding a balloon shaped like a camel and asks me to love him. I tell him I love him and stare into his eyes but I feel no love at all. He doesn't say anything, but I can tell he knows from the way he shuffles his feet and holds his own hand. "There is nothing here for me," he says before leaving. "I am alone with my camel."

I fish a cup of half-drunk espresso and a rolled up napkin out of the dirty dish bin and use them to paint a tiny baby on the floor inside my yurt. I curl my body around it and set my phone to play ocean sounds. I can't tell whether I want to cry or sleep. Eventually, I do both.

•°•

The skies these days are pink and grey, as I like them to be. The trees are warm and windblown, as I like them to be. I thumb through the book I have always wanted to read--a book unwritten--while sitting on a towel next to the waves, child in my lap. As I read, I idly pull intricate, impossible castles up from the sand all along the shore and let them slip back down as quickly as they emerge. I twist a cloud into a braid and glance up to watch it unwind. I let go of my book and it flaps its way into the most distant of trees, where it perches beyond my sight. Not that anything here is truly beyond my sight.

I am God with child. I bless my beach house. I bless my beach. I bless my child, who gurgles happy blessings back at me, for it is truly a child of mine. A child of God.

I name it ShChYNH. My love dwells within it. ShChYNH farts. It smells of promise.

When I think of my child, I imagine fresh soil, beach pines, sweet woodsmoke, waking to soft highlife music drifting in from another room. I think of immense strength restrained to the gentlest caress, virtuosity honed to the barest minimalism. I touch the face of ShChYNH. It sends shivers to my core.

My thoughts are interrupted by a dolphin's cry, followed by more. I see them flipping their way across the horizon. Seven versions of myself become fully dolphin and join them in pursuit as I look on. They place crowns of seaweed on each of my seven heads. "Hear, O waters, She is our God, She is the one," they communicate to me, with an edge of meaning I can't quite place. "Blessed is the name of Her glorious kingdom forever and ever." They continue on like this, but my mind has drifted elsewhere. I watch a cloud take the form of an angel. It passes over the sun.

• ○ •

I decide that if or when I leave the coffee shop, I will leave through the door to the left of the coffee counter. I do not know why I choose this door. While the barista is in the bathroom, I caress its handle, which says NO on it. I trace the letter N with my finger. This is definitely the door. I creep it open and I see a wall of frogs facing me. The wall crumbles into the coffee shop, knocking me over, cool and convulsing. A small one lands in my mouth, and I try to pull it out, but it is too too small. I can't find it, which makes me nervous. I had a frog in my mouth and now I cannot find it. From the ground, I ask the frogs if they would like to be loved. They do not respond. I wonder if I have offended them in some way, and I ask them if this is the case. "Fuck you," the frogs tell me. "Fuck you, bitch," they say. "Tranny faggot. Whore." Prince charming, they are not. I find a hard and dusty pink eraser in a drawer behind the coffee counter and spend the next twenty minutes rubbing them into a dark smudge that I sweep up and rub onto my face. It feels like it is rotting my skin, but I leave it. I don't know why I do this.

I knock on the bathroom door. The barista does not respond. "Did he fall in?" I think to myself. I enter. I peer under the sink, in the trash can, and push open stall door after stall door. "I could tell you things about this wallpaper," I mumble-sing to myself, "I'm like a rabbit freezing on a star." These are the only fragments of the lyric I know and it has been gnawing at me since I woke up. My teeth wear grooves into my jaw. When I open the final stall, I notice fresh scratch marks on the floor next to the hole that had been dug there previously. It looks like he did fall in. He doesn't seem to be anywhere. I think about yelling his name, but I realize I don't care, and that I'm not even sure why I bothered looking for him. Most likely out of habit.

When I go back into the coffee shop, it feels empty and arbitrary. I kick my napkin fort, but it doesn't collapse like I hoped it would. Instead, part of it just sort of crumple-tilts. I wonder if he's really gone. I think about the door again. My face itches and I scratch it. I feel the skin tear a little.

• ○ •

I am full of flowers. I pull them out of my mouth and give them to the things I want to bless with my holy light. I pull a rose from my mouth and give it to the ocean. I pull a sunflower from my mouth and give it to ShChYNH, my child, who lies at my feet, eating sand. I turn the sand in my child's mouth into mashed peas. I pull a violet from my mouth and give it to the beach. I pull an orchid from my mouth and give it to the sun. I pull the sun from my mouth and give it to myself. This is purely symbolic. The sun was mine to begin with.

I have the power of creation here, but no desire to create. My desire is understanding. I revel in it, memorizing and cataloging the endless atoms, the spark of life that glows from my surroundings. I hold my child and kiss its face. "What a small little tiny," I say to it. "You are the smallest of all the smallsmalls," I say. "Wow!" I say, "How are you the most perfect of all children and also so so much verysmall?" I kiss my child on its head. I pet its soft hair with my lips. I am in love with her softness. I am in love with all of her. This is not a love that I can end.

I have loved so many in my life, all of whom I loved briefly, for the length of our encounter. But my love for this child sticks to my ribs. I can't let go of it. I am doomed to loving ShChYNH. I am doomed to loving this small warm softness. I am a god, but I feel like until this moment, I have been a fraud. I have been offering love to anyone who comes to me, but it was barely love. That nothing-love. Just some kind of borrowed warmth. They came to me thirsty and I spit in their mouths.

I realize I am feeling negative and so I look at my child and think of the future. I create a large, horned bird with my mind. This bird takes the negative feelings from my chest and drowns them in the ocean. I bless it for doing the work of its God.

My life here is joy.

Chapter Three

I take my desires for reality because I believe in the reality of my desires.

- graffiti from the May '68 revolt in Paris

Today is the day I shall leave the coffee shop. I decided this last night, while I was God and had Godmind in my dream. In my Godmind I saw everything laid out, but now that I am not God, I no longer remember most of it. What I do remember is that today is the day I pull the handle of the No Door and take my leave for what lies beyond it.

While getting up, I accidentally destroy my yurt. Then I begin intentionally destroying it. I end up getting poked by many plastic forks but afterward I feel sweaty and good. I lick my armpit and taste the salt. It tastes like dolphins.

From across the room, I can see the barista making preparations for the day's customers. He is back, looking more stabbed than I have ever seen him before. There is one customer, a large, friendly-looking man with long hair, who has been watching me destroy my yurt with interest. I watch him back while I fish a stray pit-hair out from under my tongue. I spit it on the ground, and without breaking eye contact I scream and break the chimney off of my face.

Blood is pouring everywhere and in one swift motion, with all the anger that has pent up inside me through these years of abuse, I take five large strides, knock the barista across the face with my chimney, which feels longer, like some kind of battle staff, pull open the No Door, scream the words "PARTIAL SALINATION" (which come out of my mouth in a burst of hot light) at the frogs that have piled up there, and burst through their wet masses into the world beyond. I am not aware of the door closing behind me. I am not aware of the hole in my face or the blood on my clothes. I am not aware of the bloody wallpaper I spit out onto the fresh soil. I am only thinking of the expression on the face of the friendly-looking customer man whose eyes were locked with mine right up until I chimney-clocked the barista in the septum. He was loving me. And this is the last thought I have as I feel my legs go soft and my vision go blurry and my consciousness slip right out from under me like a wet bathmat.

Chapter Four

And over the heads of the living creatures there was the likeness of a firmament, like the colour of the terrible ice, stretched forth over their heads above.

- Ezekiel 1:22

Beyond the frogs, I have found air and sky! And suns! There are more than I remember. I count three. I must have forgotten. What suns! I have forgotten the healing power of sun. I labored and loved in the coffee shop so long that I didn't know what the suns had for me. It turns out, the thing they have for me is flowers. I take one of the flowers and place it in my hair. I use another as a boat, and slide across the ground, which is not ground but liquid of some kind. It is orange sea, it is bright pink mystery that reveals the sky and clouds clearly in its gentle waves. I see the pattern of the waves and use pollen to draw the same pattern across my stomach. I will hold it here. Maybe I will birth an ocean. Maybe I will let loose my own pink mystery upon the world.

I take my penis out and look at it. She is like a strange bird who cannot fly. "Where are your wings," I ask her. She has no answers for me. I squeeze her out of some arbitrary impulse. Still, she says nothing. I rub her with pollen for now and put her away.

I sail my flower into the air, which is barely any different from the sea or the ground or anything at all. The color pallet here is all oranges and pinks and whites, accented by the darkness of the clouds, which have a near-black purple and seem to be on the verge of delivering me with cool liquid. It has been so long. I have missed this greatly.

A creature in my flower emerges and tells me I am a sinner. I ask it what sin means and it has no answer for me. I agree that whatever it is, I am probably that thing. I have contained so much through the course of my life, though most of it from before the coffee shop seems foggy and untouchable in my mind. I rip off a large piece of petal and split it in two. I roll up each of these and place them in my nostrils. I turn my face to the sun. "I AM PROBABLY A SINNER," I yell at the largest of the suns. A god in one world could only be a sinner in another. I take a breath. I breathe in time with my heartbeat for awhile. It is too quick. I cough, then breathe normally again. The air is delicious. I sail a ways just to feel the air.

I look down from the sky just in time to see an arrow fly toward my head from somewhere forward and to my left. I duck. It misses. As I am bent down, the creature nuzzles my leg. I had forgotten it was there. I press my face into its back and it excretes a liquid from between its legs and anoints my shoulders. I try loving it and fail. Its hands are so small and look like soft black leather next to the orange-brown fur of its wrists. I rub pollen on its nose.

"Thank you," it tells me.

"For what?" I say.

"Oh," it replies.

"Oh," I say back.

We "oh" at each other back and forth for awhile, and I lose track of where we are sailing. I see the suns start to set.

"Oh."

"Oh."

"Oh."

The large sun goes down and the medium one begins to follow. Its light seems more blue, while the large one burns red. The smallest, whitest sun nearly hits the coast and turns around, heading above us again. The light changes colors through the suns' dance and I lose myself in it. If I have ever seen this before, I have forgotten. How long was I in that coffee shop? What is my life, even? I touch the creature and it grabs my finger with both its hands. It uses my finger to touch its eyeball. I pet it on the eyeball for awhile as it presses happily on my toenails. I thought I had shoes. I once had shoes. I don't care. I eat a piece of petal. It tastes like the way I want my life to be from here on out. I spit it into my palm, where it turns into a beetle. I can see my reflection in its wings. I look so, so small.

•°•

I sleep without dreams. I have no concept of time in this place. When I lift my head I see a sun, followed by a second sun just beginning to crest the lip of my boat's flower. The flower-boat's lip and its bright sun take over my vision briefly and as things come back into focus ahead I see what I can only call the Snows. I don't know how I have this name for it, because it is something I have never seen before. It is not what I would normally connect to the word "snow" or "snows," i.e. it is not droplets of freezing water crystalized around a nucleus drifting down from the clouds. It is too warm out for that. It is a thick mass of something that stretches for miles into the sky ahead. The thing it is a thick mass of is not something I can describe, because it breaks my sense of description. I do, however, know what to call it. It is the Snows and we are headed directly into its thickest point. A pure wall of amassed ineffability. As a part-time god, you would think this might be my shit, but it is, I am discovering, absolutely not my shit. I am terrified. For a moment there is nothing, then my vision goes yellow. Something unseen touches a flower to my forehead. My feet are sweating. I hear a shattering sound somewhere below me. The smell of citronella. The air is still. A voice at my ankle says something I do not understand.

"What?" I get out.

"Welcome to the Snows," it says. "You may open your eyes."

CHAPTER FIVE

There are neither skies nor oceans, neither birds nor trees—there are only signs of what can never be perceived.

- Abraham Joshua Heschel, The Holy Dimension

I am not in the Snows exactly. It's more like the Snows are in me. I feel every inch of my body filled, it leaks into every pore, every orifice. I am the Snows. The Snows are me. I know what the Snows knows. I knows it completely. I brush my hair from my face with my hand but my hand is the Snows and my hair is the Snows and my face is the Snows and what results is like a whirlpool in water. Like a stirring of undifferentiated molecules. It feels incredible. Being the Snows is not terrifying, I realize. Being myself was terrifying.

The Snows is powerful. It contains everything, every moment, every thought, every deed, every person, all life and non-life. I feel like I am being hyperbolic in my description, but the Snows is hyperbolic. It is paraboloid. I love it, it loves me, I am it, it is me, etc. It's like a control room for the universe. I see my daughter's whole life. I see her kept in a room for far too long. I see her staying the same as she grows. I see the ways she has learned how to exist in a prison. I see that I put her there. I did not remember putting her there but at some point I must have done it. None of it matters, now. I see that I am to go to her. I go to her. I go to her as the Snows. I love her as the Snows. She is the Snows. We are the Snows.

I lose track. It's like my mind contains a sharp whine that is blocking my thoughts. My thoughts fade. My thoughts are Snows. My actions are done and undone forever. All is ripple, loop, static.

Dream, reality, nothing, never, always, forever, contained, echoing into space.

The creature, who is now in the Snows, who is now part of me, who now IS me and nothing else but me, says to me, "You could become a Child of the Snows," and immediately I know this is exactly what I want, it is what I have always wanted and there is nothing more I have ever wanted. Sensing my desire, it then says, "it isn't easy. There is so much you have to do to be a Child of the Snows and it can be very difficult. I have been a Child of the Snows all my life and while I would never choose anything else, there are times I wish I wasn't a Child of the Snows."

"I understand," I tell it, and by this, I mean I tell myself, because I am the Snows and so is it and it is me. I know this thing I am choosing is not insignificant. I know that it is a huge obligation I would be taking on, to be a Child of the Snows. I also know that I want it and that this want is something I have wanted all my life. I know this decision isn't something that I would regret later. I know this is a beautiful obligation. A sacred, holy obligation. I know that there is no time when I wouldn't make this choice. "I want to become such a Child," I say into the Snows. My voice comes out a series of vibrating atoms that domino into each other in all directions, Snows against Snows, pushing across the whole of time and space and dimension and other things I don't have words for.

The Snows turns purple and rains itself. The Snows becomes a cloud and clouds me. The Snows breaks into a thousand children. The Snows requires me to answer questions and I answer them. The Snows asks me to learn and I learn. The Snows rips apart and I rip apart. I and the creature and the flower boat emerge from the ripped apart Snows. From my ripped apart self and we are holy. We are sacred. We are rain. We are children.

•°•

When I leave the Snows, I find that I have forgotten everything I knew when I was in the Snows. Something has changed inside me, though. I look at my boat-flower, at the creature, the sky, and at certain angles I notice a grain, a series of shapes. It is like what I have known as reality is starting to reveal itself as made up of letters, as characters in a holy language I can't yet comprehend. I find myself straining to make associations, to understand the immensely complex architecture at work in the creation of the world. Maybe this process of understanding is what it means to become a child of the Snows. Maybe not. I am at a loss for any sure mental footing, and so I decide this is true for now. I need something to feel true.

I don't know where we are going, but there is a character in this holy language that seems amongst the rarest of building-blocks. It looks nearly like an **X**, but off-kilter. It catches my attention when I see it on a ray of light or the sound of a bird, on an emotion or a leaf. I rub it with pollen. I decide to follow it wherever I see it. It tugs at something in me. Something deeply familiar that I've had since I was very, very young. I name it GRShM.

We continue to travel. The landscape slowly shifts from pink beach to yellow ocean to pink beach again. To forests made of people-sized leaves to deserts of hard green stone, to cities so full of fog that I am exposed to only the smallest pieces at a time before they evaporate back into oblivion. The living creature speaks to me as we travel. It tells me stories. Sometimes it is hard to understand the stories because all I can see is the holy language. The story becomes all shapes and no content. Other times I can't find the holy language anymore and I want to cry. Those times I feel like I am losing the reason for my being. I feel like I am and will always be the terrifying self I was before the Snows.

When we arrive at our destination, everything is made of various permutations of GRShM. I have become better at changing my eyes, at switching between an understanding that allows me to function in the world as a part of it and one where I can see the language beneath. On one level I see a flat field of red grass for miles, interrupted only by an immense black stone cube easily a thousand times as tall as me. On the other? GRShM GRShM GRShMGRShM GRShMGRShMGRShM. The flower lands and I run through the grass. GRShM GRShMGRShM. I approach the cube. GRShMGRShMGRShMGRShM. I touch its surface. GRShM. I lick along its flat side. GRShMGRShMGRShMGRShMGRShM. I am home.

Chapter Six

And with this I shall reveal to you a secret, which is:
Full and heaped up from line to line.
And with strong service you will understand it.

> \- Reb. Naḥman of Bratslav, "The Letter from Heaven"
> (written and sent posthumously)

"We're just a cool pair of twos," I sing into the air. "Running around the moon. Nobody's got us in trouble yet, but it's gonna happen soon." The air is crisp and pink around me. I am reclining in a chair I have made from flower dough on top of the black cube. Being a child of the snows has its perks. The creature I've been traveling with approaches me and joins in.

"Let me in your life, 'cause I've been sharpening my horns. I've been harvesting the leaves. I've been making lots of porn." I stand up and grab the creature in my arms and prepare for the big climax. At the same moment we both scream "AND I SAY" and proceed to make the noise of ten synthesizers wailing at once.

"IT'S A TALL MAN IN THE SHADOWS. IT'S A TALL MAN HE'S EATING PEOPLE. IT'S A TALL PLAN HE'S GOT FOR Uuuussssssssssssss." As we trail off, I give the creature in my arms a high five as best as I can figure out how with the anatomy it has. In return, it excretes an apple into my palm. The apple is white and speckled. I squeeze and it starts to crack. I crack it open like an egg and inside I find a stack of tiny mirrors. I rip out a few hairs from my temple and use them to tie the mirrors to my knuckles. "Thank you so much," I kiss what most likely seems to be its head.

"I love them."

I can't remember how long I've been here now. "Long" seems like a fake concept as it applies to time. I'm still seeing GRShM everywhere. He's like my special little friend. Not that GRShM has gender. It's some kind of metaphysical character of the alphabet. A nucleotide in the DNA of existence. But, one could argue that all of gender is fake and I personally think of GRShM as a sweet boy and so I use "he." Deal with it, sluts.

ANYWAY, like I was saying, I have absolutely no conception of the duration of time in which I have been hanging out with my big cube friend here. I have been treating my strange animal (?) companion as some combination of a pet and a roommate. We hooked up once. Is that weird? That's weird, I'm sorry. I was kinda in a weird place. I had been thinking about some of what I had seen in the Snows and trying to process that. There was a lot of heavy shit, I needed something else to think about, you know how it goes. So I said, "Hey there can I lick that asshole-lookin thing you got?" and it was like "YES PLEASE I've been waiting for you to ask." Aaaaaand things escalated from there. You get the picture.

And this is pretty much my life here at cube. I've got four billion and one roomies: 4 billion (exactly) GRShM and one unnameable furred creature. Rent is cheap (free) and nobody makes me love them. I love it. Effortlessly, flawlessly, I love it.

$\bullet\,^{\circ}\,\bullet$

I roll over on the pile of leaves and grass I have made on top of the cube that I am using as a bed.

"I can't sleeeeeeeeep," I whine at the creature. "Tell me a story."

The creature, who has not been sleeping, or doing anything else at all other than standing statue-still staring at the back of my head, says, "Sure. I can do that." It reaches up and pulls what seems to be a screen across my entire field of vision. It's like my whole experience of sight has become a movie. What comes next is a title card. It says "The Child Who Lived Apart."

TYFERES

CHAPTER ONE

The entire world is a very narrow bridge. The essential thing is to have no fear at all.

- Reb Naḥman of Bratslav

[Introduction; The Child Who Lived Apart]

Once, there was a rabbi who had seven children. The rabbi's goal in life was to pass the wisdom and knowledge about G-d and creation that he had amassed along to his children. Each child was considered to be not just a precious child, but a student of the great rabbi, and they would walk with the rabbi through the forest as he taught about law and creation, about the way things were and how we should best prepare for The World That Is Coming. It was said that there was little that was hidden to this great rabbi, and people would come a long way to hear him speak. As this rabbi's children grew up, one of them always separated themself from the other children. This child who lived apart from the other children would, after a long day of learning, walk a long distance back to a tiny shed they had built in the woods to sleep and prepare for the next day of learning, while the other children simply slept in the beit midrash (the house of study) their rabbi-father had built for them.

Because of this, the child (that is, the one who lived apart from the others) was socially outcast from the group, and was treated differently by them. "Sibling!" they would say to them, "Why do you live so far out in the woods? Come, stay with us and we will whisper into your ear all the mysteries of G-d while you sleep."

"No, no," they would always reply. "I am perfectly happy at my home in the woods."

[The Great Rabbi Issues a Challenge to His Seven Children]

It went on like this for quite some time until one day when the great rabbi (that is, the one who was teaching all of his children and who people came from far away to learn from) issued a challenge to all of his seven children.

"I have stocked up provisions for myself, and I am going to hide myself away inside my room for five years to study Torah," he told them. "During this time, I ask that you, my children, go out and learn what you can about the mysteries of G-d and creation. On the first day of the sixth year, I will open my door, and I expect all of you to be ready to present to me mysteries that have never before been revealed even to me. Whoever presents the greatest mystery shall have my blessing, and continue on as my successor, for I am tired of the sound of my own words. Once I have named a successor, I will no longer open my mouth except to utter words of Torah, for this is the path of the true tzaddik (righteous person)."

Having heard that, each of the children immediately made plans to travel to the farthest reaches of the known world. They began booking tickets on horses and boats, airships and ubers. The child who lived apart from the other children, however, went back to their shed in the woods and meditated. You see, this child (the one who lived apart) was skilled at traveling inside their own mind. They needed to cut down distractions to make it happen, which is why they lived so far out, but when they closed their eyes in the right setting, they could bring their mind to different times and places, to different worlds and timelines. They never knew if these were real or if they were just part of their own imagination, but the experience was so intoxicating that it absorbed all of the child's thoughts.

[The Child Goes to a Faraway Space Volcano]

The evening that their rabbi-father first closed himself in his room, the child sent their mind to the rim of a volcano on a faraway planet. As the child mind-walked around the volcano's rim, they thought about what they might be able to bring that could meet their father's challenge. No doubt some of their siblings already had things in mind that they may be able to learn.

And just as the child had that thought, a great bird came out of the sky and used its huge feet to push the mental projection of the child's body to the ground. The great bird then shrieked into the child's face, vomited jewels into their stomach and flew straight into the deepest part of the volcano.

The child cried for awhile.

The child stopped crying and began to look at the jewels. Each had a single word engraved on them. It took the better part of a day to figure out the order, but eventually the child realized they were a call for help. Whoever or whatever had engraved the jewels was trapped inside the sky and needed help. The child, who had been told from their youth that a true tzaddik (righteous person) always responds to a call for help no matter what the cost, decided the best way to find the sky was to find the shrieking vomitbird and ask for a ride into the sky to rescue the one who had sent the jewels, and so they began to climb into the volcano.

[The Child Meets the King of Fire]

The climb down into the volcano was long and arduous, and the child spent a very long time on the climb. Despite the heat, some dry grasses grew on the inside of the volcano's rim, and the child survived by eating these as they climbed down into the steamy heart of the volcano. Because they were a mental projection, they could not feel the pain of the heat, and so they eventually got to a part where everything there was on fire. It was there that they saw a great castle made entirely of glowing embers. They asked the castle guards if they had seen a great bird, but the castle guards only said, "You should speak to our king."

Once in the throne room, the child spoke to the king, whose body was entirely made of flame. The king said, "Who are you, being of skin and water who does not burn up in this place?" The child told the king about their father the rabbi and the contest and the giant bird and the messages on the jewels and everything already mentioned, etc. The king took a great liking to the child after this story and decided to help, but asked the child for one favor in return. The child agreed and the king explained that he had a child who looked almost exactly like them (that is, like the child who lived apart from the other children and was the child of the rabbi) and that their child was also made of flesh and water and yet was not burned up or boiled away by the castle. That said, the child had always stayed apart from the king's other children, who were more like the king and were made of fire and loved fire, etc. The child (that is, the child of the king who was set apart because of being made of flesh) had decided to set off to find a place in the world where they fit in, but had never come back. The king just wanted to know that his child was well. The child (that is, the child who is the hero of this story) agreed to do this, and so it was settled that they would go find the king's fleshchild and then the king would tell them about the vomitbird.

[The Child Goes Off to Find the King's Child]

The child used their mind powers to travel far and wide looking for any sign of the King's child or of the vomitbird, but couldn't find anything at all. One day, when the child was deep inside a walk-in refrigerator in the employee-only area of a Coldstone Creamery, the child (that is, the one who was the child of the rabbi and was looking for a fleshy child of a fire king) came across a coin underneath a pile of nearly empty mix-in boxes. The coin had two sides and each was engraved with a face. One face was a face that looked exactly like their own face and the other was a face that looked exactly like their own except for the presence of a volcano-shaped scar on their cheek. Out of sheer impulse, the child stuck the coin in their mouth and found themself instantly transported to a different walk-in refrigerator (this one was in a Panera). As they exited the refrigerator, they found themself face-to-face with a person who looked like a perfect mirror image of themself, only with the same volcano-shaped scar that they had seen on the coin. Immediately they took their 15 minute break and the two of them went outside to talk.

The child (our child, the rabbi's child) told the story of all that had happened to them up until now, about the rabbi, the vomitbird and the king of fire. By that time, the other child's 15 minute break was up and they had to go back to work, but the first child hung out in the parking lot playing with rocks until the other child was on their lunch break, at which time they ate broccoli cheddar soup from bread bowls, and the other child (that is, the Panera employee who was the child of the king of fire) told the story of leaving home and getting a shitty job to pay for a shitty room in a shitty house with roommates who were in a folk punk band that practiced like every single fucking day I swear it's like every day and they only know five songs but that does not stop them playing for hours and hours it is the absolute worst. They said they had thought that once they were among other beings made of flesh and water they would find someone who understood them, and wouldn't feel set apart, but instead they felt more outcast than ever.

The rabbi's child said they didn't know what a folk punk band was, but that it sounded cool, and the king's child said, "Yeah, I thought so too at first, and I did kinda like it for a little while but I'm kind of over it now."

The rabbi's child said, "That's cool, I get that, do you wanna go hang out by the river and try to throw rocks at boats," and the king's child was like "Yeah, cool that sounds fun." So they went to the river and they threw rocks at boats and when the rabbi's child got tired and sat down, the king's child sat down next to them, but sat down really close, so their thighs were touching, and the rabbi's child got tingles up their spine and blushed and the king's child grinned and said, "What?" and the rabbi's child grinned and said, "What?" and the king's child grinned and said, "Nothing" and looked down all bashful and the rabbi's child looked right at the king's child and touched the hair on the back of their neck and they made eye contact and grinned right into each other's eyes.

The two of them lived together for years. It turned out they were alike in every way, which they found out later that first day when they went skinny dipping. The only difference was the volcano scar, which got fainter and fainter over the years they lived together. They would lie in bed at night and stare into each other's eyes and it was like sleeping next to a mirror.

Chapter Two

If I am not for myself, who is for me?
But if I am for my own self [only], what am I?
And if not now, when?

- Hillel the Elder, Pirkei Avot 1:14

[The Part with a Spaceship in It]

One slow spring Sunday morning, the two children [that of the fire king and that of the rabbi] woke up late to the sun streaming in the window opposite their bed. The children had been living, sleeping, loving and working together for nearly five years at this point. They weren't really children anymore and hadn't been for a long time. In fact, when they first set out on their quest, the child who lived apart was twenty-nine. "My father will emerge from his house soon," said the child of the rabbi. "I am certain I have found the greatest piece of secret knowledge one could ever find. I believe that this piece of secret knowledge is so true and deep that even a great rabbi like my father, maybe even especially a great rabbi like my father, could never discover it unless someone like me were to bring it to him and he were to recognize it as such."

"Are you going to bring it to him?" asked the other child.

"I don't see any reason to travel a long distance to tell my father something so precious to me that he will never believe, never comprehend, much less really know, only to have him scoff at me and then never speak to me or my siblings ever again."

"I'm sorry your family is like that."

"It's okay. I do have one regret, though."

"What is that?"

"That I never helped the one who sent me that message from the sky. Through the bird's vomit."

"My father said he had information on that. We would have to go visit him."

"How do you feel about going to visit your father?"

"Fine. I don't have anything against him. He was a good father and I should visit him. I'm just not made of flames and flames are kind of the whole thing there. The whole context I grew up in feels so tangential to me. Fire is such a small part of the world."

"Sooo...let's quit our jobs and go see your dad in the volcano?"

"LET'S GO QUIT OUR JOBS AND GO SEE MY DAD IN THE VOLCANO."

And so they quit their shitty jobs and hitched a ride with a caravan headed toward the foot of the volcano. They rode mules, which was fun, because neither of them had seen a mule before.

"Wait I just thought of something," said the child of the king of fire.

"What?" said the other child.

"Is your body still sitting in the little hut near your dad's place?"

"Oh yeah, lol. Meditating."

"Do you wanna get it?"

"Nah, fuck my body."

"Gladly."

"Pffffff," the child who was very much an adult and not an actual child playfully and flirtatiously pushed the other child who was also like thirtysomething at this point and they kissed.

The caravan came to the edge of a great sea, and the volcano was on the other side of it. When they came to it, it was icy cold and held a reflection of the moon. As they began the trek around the lake, they saw three blue and red birds that were really pretty and a hovering violet spaceship shaped like a pyramid. A yellow cloud drifted across it slowly and the whole scene was reflected in the lake below in gentle shades of blue. It was amazing. They tried to get close to it but it was probably like fifty feet above the ground and not going anywhere. They left quickly because they were worried they might get squished if it landed. The birds were regular birds, just pretty ones.

[The Two Children Meet a Leg and Journey to Fur Mountain]

Eventually, the two not-children left the spaceship behind and took the direction that seemed the weirdest. As the landscape got stranger, they came across a naked leg planted upside-down in the ground. It was tan and covered in hair and had a small mouth on the big toe from which it expelled gas in airy moans that sounded like it was saying "ah." The gas was white and smelled almost exactly like an adult book store.

"Uh, hello?" said one of the children.

"Ah how ah can I help you ah," said the leg.

"We are looking for the volcano where the fire king lives," said the child of the fire king. "Do you know which way it is?"

"Ah ah ah ah," said the leg. It bent back and forth, and as it did this it became clear that there were two long flaps of loose skin that seemed to dangle and sway limply as it moved, like ineffective, boneless, wrinkly arms. It pointed the bottom of its foot this way and that like it was looking for something, though it did not seem to have eyes. "Ah you will need to go to the face on ahhh the other side of Fur Mountain and talk ahah to the Rainbear ah."

"You mean the mountain over there?" the child pointed to a mountain that seemed to be covered in brown fur.

"Ahhhhhhhhhhhhhhhhhhhhhhhhhhhhhhhhhhhhhhhhhhhhhhhhhhhh

hhhhhhhhhhhhhhhhhhhhhhhhhhhhhhhhhhhhhhhhhhhhhhhhhh
hhhhhhhhhhhhhhhhhhhhhhhhhhhhhhhhhhhhhhhhhhhhhhhhhhh
hhhhhhhhhhhhhhhhhhhhhhhhhhhhhhh,"said the leg as it let out
an enormous cloud of gas that gave them a head rush.

"Thank you," said the child of the Rabbi, the one who had
lived apart and whose body was still meditating far, far away.

And so they walked on until they got to the mountain made of fur.
As they got closer, they realized that, in fact, the fur was not brown
at all. Each strand was a different color, this one bright pink, this
one a dull yellow, that one emerald green, another baby blue. This
created an effect of brownness until you got close enough to see the
colors. The fur was long and curly and seemed well-conditioned
and shiny as it moved gently in the wind. They began to climb,
and as it got steeper they had to grip the fur to keep from sliding
backwards. Eventually, they got to a place where it leveled off a bit
before ascending to the final peak. They used this less-steep region
to journey around the side of the hairy mountain until they came to
a salty river by which they set up camp.

"Thank you for coming with me all this way," said the child of the
Rabbi.

"You are my person," said the child of the fire king. "I will
support you as I can and love you with all my heart. I will do what
feels best for you and for me so that we can be our best selves for
each other. I will be by your side, yes, of course, as I can and as is
needed. I will also follow my own path and let you follow yours as
we need. We are born and we die and in the time in between we
must find a way to help others live in a way that is beautiful and
as free from pain and hardship as possible with the ideal that we

too might be able to live in a way that is beautiful and as free from pain and hardship as possible. When I see you, you remind me of that so deeply in the core of my being that I forget anything else. It is inspiring and almost overwhelming. I get so full of it I can't do anything but rededicate myself wholly to that project. And so, yes, I will come with you because you make me feel like I can accomplish the only thing ever worth accomplishing."

"Thank you," said the child of the Rabbi, wiping away tears. "That is all I could ever ask for. I feel like we match so well and I don't really know what I want from life, because most of what I have felt has been alienation up until I met you. I did the things I did and made the choices I made in order to keep myself distracted from a resigned feeling of bleakness that the alienation had created in me. You seem to actually know, to have a clear perspective on things. I don't have that, I don't know if I will ever have that, but if I can help you accomplish what you need to accomplish, maybe I'll start to find out for myself. When I got this message from this guy, I only wanted to help him sort of on instinct. My dad taught us certain things: *Tzedek* (justice), *Tzedekah* (redistribution of capital), *Mishpat* (law), *Chesed* (lovingkindness). I think these are fine things to live by. But I'm still figuring out what they mean to me. Or even if they are a worthwhile framework at all. On my good days, though, it's like I can see through your eyes. I look out at the world and feel such an overwhelming sense of *chesed* for everything and I want to feel like that for the rest of my life. And maybe if I try to live like that all the time, even when I can't feel it, maybe that's how I can figure out how to become the person I want to be."

[The Children Meet the Rainbear]

That night, the two children (who, I feel like I should again emphasize, are absolutely not children, but grown adults who are well into their adulthood), had some really really good sex. It was super hot. The child of the rabbi does this like, mischievous thing and the whole sex becomes like an adventure, like with the fur all over the ground they were like wrestling and the child of the fire king pushed the child of the rabbi on the ground and put their toe in the child of the rabbi's mouth and said "ah ah ah" like it was the foot putting out gas and the child of the rabbi cracked up and said "oh my fucking G-d nooooooo" and they both laughed and laughed and rolled around in the fur and the child of the rabbi pushed the child of the fire king almost entirely into a shallow part of the river and sat on their face and they started eating out their asshole and then giving them head and then there was like a whole petplay thing for a bit except instead of pet/owner it was more like pet/G-d and then G-d peed on the pet's face.

The next morning, they woke up and washed themselves in the salty river and it was really good for their hair. They waded through the river, which seemed to have calmed its flow to a level they could more easily wade across. About ten minutes after they got across the river, they felt the ground moving beneath them and heard a deep, sad-sounding voice that seemed to vibrate through their whole bodies.

"Hello little children," said the voice. "I," it sighed, "am the Rainbear."

"Um, hello!" shouted the rabbi-child. "Where…uh…where are you?"

At that, a massive face leaned over their heads. It looked like the face of an enormous, sleepy bear covered in the same rainbow fur they had been hiking through. It had one grey eye and one yellow eye and there was a river pouring from each one. As he leaned over them the rivers became waterfalls. Fur mountain was not just a mountain, it seemed.

"I suppose I should show you my face, it will make communication easier I suppose," sighed the Rainbear in his sleepy-sad tones.

"Can I just say," said the fire-child, "That you are like, absolutely amazing?"

"I suppose you can," the Rainbear sadly smiled.

"Why are you crying," asked the child of the Rabbi.

"I am crying," sighed the Rainbear, "because the world."

"Yeahhhhh," said both children at the same time, nodding sadly.

"Can I tell you a story?" said the Rainbear.

"Actually, we would love that," said the child of the fire king, looking at their partner and then back to the Rainbear.

"This story," said the Rainbear, "is called The Tale of the Weird Old King."

The story took a long time to tell, as the story was long, and Rainbear spoke slowly and sighed frequently. I'm going to tell it much more quickly and with the sighs removed to make it a little bit easier, but remember that this is all coming out in the voice of the Rainbear.

Chapter Three

Nine hundred and three types of death were created in the world.... The most difficult of all these types of death is croup, while the easiest is the kiss of death. Croup is like a thorn entangled in a wool fleece, which, when pulled out backwards, tears the wool.... The kiss of death is like drawing a hair from milk. One should pray that he does not die a painful death.

- Talmud Bavli, Berakhot 8a:13

[Introduction; The Weird Old King]

Once, there was a weird old king who tried to bury his own kingdom in the earth. He talked to all his advisors and commanders and overseers and saw to it that the royal army and all of the forced laborers were to dig holes in the earth the size of everything in the kingdom. Horse-shaped holes would contain the horses and bank-shaped holes would contain the banks. And, like this, slowly the whole kingdom existed in holes, sunk into the earth. Of course, animals that live in holes cannot get out to feed themselves, and so many of them died. Plants and crops that are in holes and cannot get sun, cannot grow and so, many of them died. The king had his men close up all the holes over top. In this way, the whole village was buried. The things that were alive were buried alive. The king had his closest advisor, a prophet named Acher, bury him (the weird, old king) last. Acher told the king, as he had from the very beginning of the king's weird obsession, that this was a bad idea, but the king commanded him, and so Acher buried the king alive. With this, Acher was alone. The whole kingdom no longer existed. And so Acher made the decision to go out and see the world.

Acher was a prophet of a sun god named Rapha. Rapha had no temple in the land (not even a buried temple) and so Acher made the decision to go and seek out other acolytes of Rapha in order to better dedicate himself to his chosen deity. He roamed the countryside in the sunlight, and slept in the moonlight until, one day, he came upon a big city, much bigger than the city he had just buried. Surely, he thought, there would be a temple to Rapha here. As he searched the city, he began noticing something that made him concerned.

He came to a well, where a woman was working. "Excuse me, can I ask you a question?" he asked her.

"Absolutely," she replied. He realized when she turned to him that her eyes were made of oak. She seemed to be able to see just fine.

"Is there a temple to Rapha in this city?"

The woman belched and a bird climbed out of her mouth. "Excuse me," the bird said.

"No problem," replied the woman and turned back to her work at the well.

Acher went to walk away, and in his confusion, he stepped into a second well. A bird flew down to him, said, "Excuse me," and stepped into his open mouth.

Acher mumbled a prayer to Rapha for comfort.

[Acher Meets Shimon and They Fuck]

At the bottom of the well, Acher found a tunnel. He crawled through it, his shirt getting muddy and sticking to his skin. At the end of the tunnel, there was a piece of wood blocking the way, and so Acher slowly dug it out, using his fingers to scratch away at the mud. Behind the wood, there was a series of iron bars, which he dug out as well, one by one. Behind the iron bars were a set of bones, placed gently in a pocket in the earth. Behind the bones was a hole, with a face looking at him. The face was scarred and grisled. It had coffee-and-tobacco breath. The face was attached to a body and together the face and the body were called Shimon.

Shimon was taller than Acher, and didn't say a word as he brought him through a series of tunnels and into a heated room with a fire and what must have been a chimney tunneled up to the surface. There were rugs there covering the dirt floor and an overstuffed chair. Shimon stripped off Acher's muddy clothes and washed him in a basin. Acher touched the man's hair as Shimon slid his rough hands along Acher's legs. Acher kissed Shimon's coffee and tobacco mouth, and in that kiss, Acher felt the stresses of his journey so far flow out of him. Shimon picked him up and dried off his body with a soft chamois and carried him to the overstuffed chair by the fire, where he sat down with Acher on his lap. Shimon wet his hand and slid it, finger by finger, slowly, gently inside Acher's asshole. Acher felt him grip something that had been lodged there and pull. It took some effort and it felt like it was attached to Acher's skeleton when Shimon pulled on it, but it did not hurt. Then, with a satisfying pop, it loosened. It was like a plug had been pulled. Acher moaned and a slippery blue dog came out of him into Shimon's hairy arms. That was the last image Acher saw before he passed out.

When Acher woke up, he was in a field of flowers with brown petals and black centers. Their stems and leaves were white. The sky was magenta and there were sixteen green suns. He was wearing silk pants with an elastic waist. They had one red leg and one yellow leg. The cuffs were blue. He found a note taped to his naked chest. He assumed it was from Shimon. Inside it said this:

Dear Shibboleth,

I traveled to the ocean and it was so beautiful that I needed to get rid of it. Nothing should be like that. Life has too much suffering for such beauty to exist. The contrast is too fucking much. I pulled out my Google Pixel 4 and called the damn cops. They came and tried to arrest the beach but their handcuffs just went through the sand, and the water just slipped right out. They got angry and tried to beat up the waves but the waves just splashed and played and beat back at them. This made the cops madder than ever. They told their boss, who told her boss, who told his boss, who told his boss, who told G-d and so G-d got rid of the beach. Then the cops arrested me and put me in jail. My cellmate was a bobcat kitten who missed his mom and tore my flesh every night with his claws. 50,000 people tried to kill me by projecting their evil thoughts. There was no beauty to be found anywhere. "That's more like it," I said. "That's more like it."

Love you forever,
Fire and Hail, Snow and Smoke

Acher stood up from the field and headed on to the next town.

[Acher Encounters a Lion]

Acher roamed for a very long time until he came across two people on their hands and knees, vigorously digging around inside the corpse of a lion with both hands. "Greetings," he said to them.

"Lion," replied the taller one.

"Lion to you too," said Acher.

"No," said the shorter one. "This is a lion."

"Was," said Acher.

"Was," agreed the taller one, without looking up from his digging.

"Is there a town anywhere near here?" said Acher.

"Nope," replied the shorter one.

"City," said the taller one.

"There's a city?" asked Acher.

"City," said the shorter one.

"Which way to the city?" said Acher.

"Ahead," said the shorter one.

"Ahead," agreed the taller one..

At no point did either actually look up or make eye contact with any part of Acher.

"My ahead or your ahead," said Acher.

The shorter one laughed.

"We've all got a head," said the taller one.

"Even this lion. Dead. Got a head." said the shorter. He moved the lion's head around on its limp neck, possibly pretending it was a puppet, but the attempt was too brief and feeble to be interpreted successfully.

[Acher Comes to Another City and Purchases a Salamander]

Acher walked on from there until he saw a city on the horizon. When he entered it, he saw it was filled with all kinds of sights. Beautiful temples loomed above the other structures. An enormous marketplace with merchants selling all the most luxurious technology. Acher purchased a small cage containing an even smaller salamander that breathed fire whenever asked. Perfect for lighting rollies and campfires on cold nights while travelling. It ate peas, so Acher bought a large sack of those as well.

He asked the merchant he bought them from if there was a temple to Rapha in the city. The merchant had a face netted in red marks that looked as if he had fallen asleep face-first on a chain-link fence. He replied with a series of wheezes. Acher was unsure if they were speaking the same language or if this was simply how the merchant spoke. Acher replied by letting out a short string of wheezes, just in case. The merchant reached out and took Acher's hand.

The merchant led Acher through the city by his hand, their fingers interlocked. They went down back alleyways and up flights of stairs that seemed to go nowhere, only to turn at the last second into an unseen elevated walkway. Eventually, they came to a large temple, but the merchant pulled Acher right past it and toward the edge of the city. When they came to the edge of the city, the merchant wheezed a few sweet nothings in Acher's ear and brought him up a set of stairs to the top of the city wall. They sat down and dangled their legs over the edge and watched the sun set over the horizon. The merchant leaned over and kissed Acher, pushing something into Acher's mouth with his tongue before standing up and jumping off the wall to the outside of the city. Acher was at a loss. He pulled the thing out of his mouth and saw it was a small rolled up piece of paper. He unrolled it and written on it was one word. It said "excrement." Acher stayed in the town two more nights but did not find what he was looking for, and so he moved on.

The first night after leaving the city, while Acher was sitting beside his campfire, a ghost appeared to him. It was the ghost of the Weird Old King. The ghost choked him until he passed out. When Acher came to, it was morning.

[Acher Renounces Rapha and is Consumed by an Ooze]

Acher woke up, got dressed, tore his clothes and renounced Rapha. He waved his bare penis in the air and touched his nipples. A grey ooze seeped up from cracks in the ground, developed three mouths on three long stalks and attached itself to his right index finger, his left index finger and the tip of his penis. It swallowed and coated his entire body. It smoothed out over his skin and changed the look of Acher's features. This creature that had assumed Acher spoke with Acher's mouth as it said, "We are a new creature." It was not speaking to anyone in particular. Acher-creature dug a hole and buried itself in the ground. Nothing was to be done from there.

Chapter Four

You will again have compassion upon us.
You will hurl all our sins into the depths of the sea.

- Micah 7:19

[The Children Leave Fur Mountain]

"Huh," said the child. "I mean, thank you for that story. Was there something you wanted us to learn from it?"

"There is so much to be learned from this story I have told you. For example, the Ooze is about what can happen to us if we let our pain turn us into creatures that project that pain onto others. If we become persecutors as a way to avoid being victims. That right there, I just enlightened your eyes with a little bit, in order to somewhat understand and comprehend the extent to which these things reach. But the things are still sealed in utter concealment, for all the stories that I tell are very, very high above human comprehension and hidden from the eye of all living creatures, etc," said the Rainbear in his sleepysad drone of a voice.

"You almost sounded like my dad right there for a second," said the child of the great rabbi.

"So," said the Rainbear. "You want to find the volcano."

"Yes!" said the fire-child. "Do you know it?"

"It's right there," said the Rainbear. And sure enough, what was clearly the volcano was actually super close and they just hadn't looked around really since they had crossed the river.

"Oh!" said the rabbi's child. "Thank you!"

"I hope your travels go well," intoned the Rainbear as his head sunk back out of their field of view. They could still kind of see up his nose.

[The Children Visit Fire-Child's King-Dad]

The children went on from there to the volcano. In the volcano they found the King of Fire, who hugged and kissed his child.

"You have grown so much older!" he said. "Will you come stay here with me in the city of fire?"

"No," said the child. "You see, I have found love." At this, the child looked at the other child.

"Oh," said the king. "Ohhhhhhhhhhhhhhhhhhhh." There was a long silence.

"Do you have the information about the vomitbird you promised me all those years ago?" said the child of the Rabbi nervously.

"Oh, yes," said the king. "Yes, I suppose I can give you this."

The king gave them a link that showed them how to jailbreak an iPhone and get a weird app that would surround them with a bubble and float them into the sky, all the way up into the cloud domain of the vomitbird.

"Uh, I only have a flip phone," said the child of the Rabbi.

"I've got an android?" said the child of the fire king, and pulled a small robot out of their backpack.

"Hello, how can I help y'all?" said the android with an Alabama drawl.

"Oh one second," said the fire king and rummaged around in the cushions of his fire-throne. "Here," he said and placed a gold ring around his lips. "Plumbaby," he said and the words came out visible in the air, made out of black fire.

"Thank you," said the android and sucked the black fire into its mouth.

Immediately, a bubble formed around the children and they began to float up into the air.

"I love you," said the fire king from below, and the words came out in black fire.

"I appreciate that," said his child, crying a little as they drifted off. "I can see you mean well. But you don't even know me. You never have. So who is it that you love?"

The fire king said something else, but they couldn't hear it, as they were pretty far up now. They only saw the fire, etching symbols in the air. The child felt glad they said what they said, but also sort of like an asshole.

[The Children visit the Cloud Realm of the Vomitbird]

The bubble floated the children up and up until they reached a massive cloud that looked like a mountain. The bubble took them deep inside this cloud until a space opened up and there was a golden-pink cloud shaped like a bird's nest. In the bird's nest was the bird they had seen before. The bird that had vomited in front of the Rabbi-child literally only once and thus earned the unfortunate nickname Vomitbird.

The bubble perched on the side of the nest. The vomitbird woke up, looked at them like it just absolutely did not care at all, and lazily flew off.

"Well, fuck," said the child of the rabbi.

"Sweetie, look," said the child of the fire king. In the spot where the vomitbird once laid there was a stack of paper. It looked like it had been printed off a dot-matrix printer and was all connected into one long sheet and had the little side bits with the holes in them you can tear off.

"I think these are letters," said the child of the rabbi, picking up the stack and starting to glance through. "Or a journal of some kind."

"Read them to me!" said the child of the fire king, settling down and getting comfy in the cloud-nest.

"Oh, yeah! Okay, here we go."

MALXUS

Chapter One

But when do we exist?

   - Rainer Maria Rilke, "Sonnet to Orpheus no. 3", trans. David Young

Today when the room was Yellow, I found a part of it I hadn't looked at in awhile. It had a number of my things in it, things that aren't important when I'm not looking at them, which is usually, especially in this corner of the room, which I hadn't looked at in awhile. This was happening when the room was Yellow. In this part of the room, I found a small girl holding onto a wire. She was too small to talk, the way that I was once too small to talk but also in a different way. She was a girl I could tell because of the way she was so hungry, eating at that wire. I pulled her off and stripped some of the rubber coating off the wire and gave it to her separately to eat so she didn't chip her tooth or brain on the electricity there. I miss her. It hasn't been Yellow in awhile, and after it was Yellow today I lost her and she ran away to another part of the room I don't usually look at, I'm assuming. But it makes me happy knowing there's another girl in here with me, even if she's a very small one who's smaller than me. I'd like to be small again, but I don't think I could ever be as small as her.

I told my friends about the Yellow today and the girl. This was later, when the room was Blue. My friends didn't say anything, they never say anything, but they are soft, and possibly also too small to talk. I'm big enough to talk pretty much always. I'm a big big talker girl. But when the room was Blue, I sat on the bed and told my friends, who were all different things that have been nice to me while I'm here in the room. They were nice again, but too quiet, everything is too quiet so I like making sounds, music and being a big big talker.

A day goes like this: Green, Yellow, Red, Orange, White, Black (none), Second Green, Orange-White, Blue-Green, Blue, Silver-Like-the-Moon, Cherry-Red, White again and Pets-colored. Then it's Green again and Yellow and the whole thing again. Once it was Pink and I miss that. Maybe it was Red or Cherry Red and I woke up and squinted and saw Pink but I don't know, it was Pink-Pink if I remember it right, it didn't seem Red or Cherry Red. I miss that. It has never been Purple or Violet or Indigo or anything like that. No Fuchsia or Lavender or Periwinkle or Burgundy or any kind of thing somebody might call Purple. I wonder if when I have lived long enough that the room might be Purple. It seems possible to me, but I'm a dreamer and I know not everyone will believe like I do.

I'm making a journal as a joke. Today I thought it would be funny to make a journal as a joke. There's a screen here, I can press keys and make words. It doesn't do anything, I just make words and the words stay there, but I figure I can make as many as I want. I haven't found a maximum amount of words I can put in this because sometimes I'll just fall asleep on the keys at Cherry-Red and wake up in the middle of Pets-Colored and the letters will still be going so I don't think there's an end. So I decided to make this as a joke to myself when I'm a lot of days later so I can think it's funny to see what I'm saying now.

DEAR DAYSLATER SELF:

I made this journal for u I think you're going to be so beautiful × × Δ I love u

Wow.

Dayslater Self,

You make me smile just thinking of you. I bet if we got together it would be so much sound and words in the room because we're both such big big talker girls. I think you're pretty. I wish you could write back to me but I don't think that can happen, even though now that I thought about it there's a small part of me that hopes when I wake up I will see words in here that you wrote back to me. I don't talk to other big big talkers EVER, so it feels like this might be my best chance. Maybe this can be another thing I believe in. I believe in Pink, I believe in Purple and I believe in you, dayslater self.

You know the corner of the room that's all the smells? Today during Green I took all my clothes off and got all naked and put my clothes there in that corner and peed on them bc I was thinking about it, and I realized I've never done that before and why not? It turns out the why not is itchy, so I probably won't do that again but now I know how to make itchy in case I need that one, so I think today has been a good day but I should have let them dry off instead of just staying itchy, but now they're not itchy, now they're just dry and smells.

Today I slept from Red to Orange and from Blue to Silver-Like-the-Moon and that is a lot less sleeps than usual. I wasn't doing much, I mostly stayed w the friends in bed and talking to them and during SSecond Green I picked out the food for me for the whole day, though I think maybe tomorrow I would like to have food earlier like during first Green or Yellow if there aren't any small girls to watch during Yellow. Oh! Maybe if small girl is there at Yellow again tomorrow eating the cord, I can eat the cord with her or my regular food instead of the cord bc I want to be okay. Yes, I will eat my regular food and I will say, "Small girl! How is your cord rubber today?" And she will eat her cord rubber and I will say, "You certainly seem to be enjoying it!!" And I will laugh like I laugh with my other friends or with myself sometimes, though I guess every time I laugh it is with myself.

Why am I so different from my friends will be my thing I write about tomorrow, I just decided. I will write about why my friends are such small quiet quiet when I am big loud. Maybe I will try being small and quiet tomorrow for a color or two. Or a whole day, but that seems like too much for now. I will start small, because I actually did start small in my life. Dayslater self, are you bigger than me? I used to get bigger all the time but now I have been the same big as the big box when I'm in it for a long long long long long time. For way longer than the time when I was still getting biggerbigger every day. Would I bigger again if I had a bigger box?

It is getting to be White again and I should sleep or I will miss too much of Pets-colored, which feels bad. I like to be able to give Pets-colored good attention bc I think it must feel sad when I sleep all during it bc I know I wouldn't like that. I'm going to sleep now, so I love you small girl and I love you dayslater Self and I love you my friends and I love you Pets-colored. I hope u all see Puuuurple × • ° • ¶¶¶

• ° •

Oh beautiful dayslater self!

It is tomorrow now and I am closer to you than I have ever been! It's so exciting to know that soon enough I will be the self that is dayslater & could be my own other talker! Wow°^° • ××Δ • °!! I cannot! believe it! And I'm the believer, even! Anyway, my beautiful, I am writing to you from what I think is the end of a beautiful first Green, lying in bed and thinking of Yellow and my food date with small girl coming ahead! I have decided the small girl's name that I will call her. I like having names for my friends, and since she is the newest one of them, the only one who I hadn't given a name, I figured it was about time. I asked my other friends what would be a good name. When I named them I thought of all kinds of beautiful things to name them. They are called, in order from biggerest (besides me) to smallsmall: Marjorie With the Ears, Elvis, Nana, Cabin-boy, Songy, Tremaine of the Antler, Christlike Reverence, Camshaft, Leroy, Salad-Bar and Buttz. I love them all so much and ohmygosh you should see what a small small smallgirl I have of a friend in Buttz. Wow ×∆• •. So very tinysmall! Anyway, when I meet my small girl today for rubber lunch, I have decided her name will be Annmarie Loudermilk because she is perfect & deserves the best name I can think of, which right now is Annmarie Loudermilk.

I've been thinking about why I am different from my friends today. My friends are things that have been nice to me while I'm here in the room and I think I have been nice to me except sometimes but mostly always nice to me, so I would be a friend too. But my friends are, like I said before, not talkers. So quiet. Even Annmarie Loudermilk is quietquiet though she moves around on herself by her own like the way I do too. I'm having a lot of trouble figuring out how I fit in with them. I'm a namer and they're not, I'm loud loud and I'm a mover and they're not (except Annmarie Loudermilk who is a mover too but so so quiet so it's different). I would like to be more like my friends I think sometimes but most of the time I'm glad I get to do all the things I do, and it's what makes me special, the way Marjorie With the Ears has those ears that, let me tell you, NOBODY has!! I'm a believer and there are things like that that I am that I don't even KNOW if my friends are because I have to have their parts of the conversation be quiet and so I make up different answers to the things I ask them every time. Which I do for myself too, but when I do it for myself it's also the real answer unless I want it to not be for a joke. I miss small girl. Also! I don't want to interrupt, but it just turned Yellow and my food is already out, I'm so excited.

I guess to make this part be over, I would say that I am mostly different but the same as my friends but am more different from them than I would sometimes like to be, but also there is the argument about specialness and my having it and how that's good. Which is a solid argument and probably the one I'm deciding on, but I always let myself undecide later too, just in case. Wow! I just realized you probably know whether or not I undecided because you LIVE in later!!!! Hahahah oh my GOSH. I'M SPENT IN LAUGHTER RIGHT NOW√Δ√× • × • ¶

OKAY. Sorry about that outburst, SHEW, I was so loud right there! I will write you more soon, probably around either Black (none) or Orange-White after next sleep if I'm feeling particularly a way or I find another thing to do that I haven't done yet in the room. There's the part I don't look at much, the one I mentioned before during lastYellow, and I was thinking that I could look at it a lot, which would be a newish thing for me.

Oh! Goodbye beautiful>˜ ˜ ˜ ˜ ×
Wow I love you??

P.S. I just had the FUNNIEST THOUGHT! What if I had a name or made one for me???? Haha I'm laughing so much about this, what a good joke I could make! Ok ok I just had to share hahaha!°ΔΔ •

• ° •

Dear dear dear dear dear dear Dayslaterself,

Do you have a name? I mean yes, actually I definitely know that you do, because I HAVE ONE NOW and that means that definitely yes actually you have one too because you are me after now. I have decided that my name from now on will be Muriel Claudia Edeltraud-

Lilybridge. I am going to say the whole thing every time because oh my gosh oh my gosh what a beautiful name! I thought of this name to cheer myself up because I was about to eat my food at Yellow today and was waiting for Annmarie Loudermilk to show up for our date and she WAS NOT SHOWING and I was waiting and waiting and I felt myself getting too too sadsad for my own good! It was so silly, I was sadsadsupersad and not eating and ended up making water in my eyes and then peed all over myself and sat in it and blooded my legbottoms with the silly sandpaperstick I named Jaems even though Jaems is NOT a thing in the room that has helped me and does NOT need a name like why would I name the thing that gives me a badtime after I have a badtime? Anyway, I was stinging and hurting and itchy and hunger all at the same time but then Yellow was over and it was RED and I was like Oh You Silly What! And so I used the water from my eyes that I made (at least I had the sense to collect it like I try to do!) and cleaned me all up! I got naked and washed first clothes with the new eyewater along with myself and put on second clothes and decided I needed to cheer me up. And so I thought about what I sent you yesterday and got soso excited about my selfname!! And that is the big story about how I am called Muriel Claudia Edeltraud-Lilybridge Δ^Δ^×× • ° •

Wow! What a tale! And so now it is almost all the way to Orange and I have eaten my food all by my own self for sure, but I had thoughts about why Annmarie Loudermilk didn't come and I think it is probably too much traffic for such a small girl! There are so many ways to get lost or slowed down if you are smallsmall and I know this because I put my face down by the ground and looked around the whole room and wow! There's so much!! Like my eyes are big and not so littletiny and still! it was hard to see much at all because there are soso many floor things like my food pieces and my food plastic and the bed pile for sleep and my friends and like even just Marjorie With the Ears must be way big to see and so I have decided that

Annmarie Loudermilk got lost roaming around thinking about lunch and cordrubber in my corner with her wonderful new friend Muriel Claudia Edeltraud-Lilybridge. I am sure we will reconnect at a later date, but I don't want to make a date for it because what if it was a surprise to get to see my goodfriend Annmarie Loudermilk? That would be good!!!!!!!!

I can't wait to see Pets-colored today!!! It is soso long, maybe 3 sleeps from now, but for now it is time for sleep one and so I will say beautiful goodbye to you now dayslater self! OR SHOULD I SAY DAYSLATER MURIEL CLAUDIA EDELTRAUD-LILYBRIDGE??

!!!!!!

I love you dayslater Muriel Claudia Edeltraud-Lilybridge! Remember Pink is real! May u see Purple for finally!!! ° • Δ • °°

• ° •

Hi Dayslater MCE-L,

It is now Second Green and I just had first sleep and more food. I am trying to eat three foods between sleeps and to take care of myself like that. But it is hard sometimes! I realized when I was eating that I am now dayslater to oldself that wrote the first diary. I read first diary and gosh, I feel so much love for oldself Muriel Claudia Edeltraud-Lilybridge!! She didn't even know that was her name yet!!!

I talked to Tremaine of the Antler and Songy before first sleep about wishing I had another talker here. You and Oldself are nice and I love you both so much but there is more things I want and I don't even know what they are!! I'm confused a LOT and maybemaybe it would help to talk about my confused. I don't know, Muriel Claudia Edeltraud-Lilybridge, I don't know! Why do I think about this so much?? I guess it will be a thing I figure out later. Maybe you have figured it out, Dayslater! If so, and you figure out a way to tell me, please please let me know oh gosh that would be so so good!!!!!

I drew a picture of Salad-Bar today, she sat still so well for me and was very very good while I drew! What a good friend!!!! I will probably write more later today byebye for now I love youΔ • ×°°

• ° •

Hi,

It's Silver-Like-the-Moon and I am having the feeling. I hate the feeling so much I wish I wish it could be all done. All done forever. All done all done. I'm so big today. Soso big. I was in the corner of the room where I found Annmarie Loudermilk and I found another small girl. It wasn't Annmarie Loudermilk or any of the other friends, she was her own small girl. She didn't look like Annmarie Loudermilk, who is soft-looking with the smallhair all over and big kind of ears. She looked like me. Like you. She is me but smaller. So small. Impossibly small. She looked up at me and I had the feeling again a little bit and then I was having the feeling a lot a lot and laid on the ground because I think the feeling decided that I am on the ground. It is less than it was because I am now able to write this not like before but it's still a lot so much. I almost thought the feeling was gone forever but it's back and I hate it. I am afraid to look in the corner because I am scared the new small girl will be there and I am scared the new small girl won't be there and I am scared about the feeling being here because it's too much and stays when I don't want it here stays too long too long. It's Silver-Like-the-Moon and I am afraid plus the feeling. I am going to be on the ground again for awhile. I don't know if I can catch any of the eyewater this time.

I know you can't help me probably but help please please please

please please please pleasepleasp

• ° •

Dear dearest best dayslater darling Muriel Claudia Edeltraud-Lilybridge,

Oh wow! It's so good to write to you!!!! It's been a day or more, I stopped paying attention to colors for a little while but it has been SO SO long too long too long since I wrote to you. Pets-colored came in maybe once maybe twice and it was so nice having it with meeee!!! I love my Pets-colored. Right now it is Blue-Green, and will probably turn Blue soon. I am soso sorry my last diary was so scary, Dayslater Muriel Claudia Edeltraud-Lilybridge!! It has been a WILD ride, that's for sure. I am sosoSOso glad to have all of my friends who help me so much!!!!! Before I wrote this, I spent time with Salad-Bar and Marjorie With the Ears and Christlike Reverence, who is mostly REALLY nice to me because I looked inside her for awhile and at some of the words in her. One of the parts I really liked even though I don't get all of every one of her words but she said this:

> [1]Peace, troubled soul, whose plaintive moan
> Hath taught each scene the note of woe;
> Cease thy complaint, suppress thy groan,
> And let thy tears forget to flow:
> Behold, the precious balm is found,
> To lull thy pain and heal thy wound.

Also, Marjorie With the Ears was very soft and Salad-Bar and me put our noses together and I gave her lotsandlotsandlots of head kisses for being so nice and softtttttt. THANK YOU SO MUCH

MY FRIENDS!!! THANK YOU SO MUCH DAYSLATER MURIEL CLAUDIA EDELTRAUD-LILYBRIDGE!!! WE'RE GONNA SEE THAT PURPLE I KNOW IT I KNOW IT I KNOW IT √•×¶∆∆∆°•°∧•⋀•••°⋀°°

Chapter Two

In the spiritual vacancy of life something may suddenly occur that is like the lifting of a veil at the horizon of knowledge.

— Abraham Joshua Heschel, The Holy Dimension

Dearest dayslater Muriel Claudia Edeltraud-Lilybridge!!!

I miss you so much! It is wonderful to talk to you my lovelydearest friend of all friends!!! When can we finally see each other, I do not know, but gosh oh gosh I hope it is soon! Lately things have been fine. I had the feeling but the feeling did not come back and the small girl who is NOT Annmarie Loudermilk did not come back. I even got up a bigbig courage and got myself to be a strongest girl and look to see if she was still there and she was not. Sometimes I wonder if the things I see are really things that I see or if they are not, but I also am thinking that what is the difference, really because if I see a thing then it is just the same as all the things I see because maybe none of the things I see are real and maybe they all are and maybe just some are but who can know? Not me, that is most for sure. Maybe you know, D.L.S. (dayslater self)? If you do that would be wow so fantastic if you told me, but I get it, I know that you maybe haven't figured out how to do that because I know I haven't figured out how to do that or I would be telling my pastself version of Muriel Claudia Edeltraud-Lilybridge that she should be REAL careful about new types of small girls and getting the feeling again WOW that would have been so helpful, I wish I could be that helpful!

I am the bestest of friends to myself basically always except sometimes. Isn't that amazing? I think it is amazing. OH and I drew a story about two of my friends GOSH it's so funny. I'm sure you saw it because you are in the dayslater where you have already made it but GOSH I hope you read this and remember how funny and good it is.

Right now I am eating firstmeal past secondsleep and it is Black (none), which is a good color for being all restful with friends but not sleep like a fullsleep. I am writing you this letter during this time and I think it is a good time for writing it because I know how to do that during Black (none), which is nice. I am thinking about really out there things lately! Like I saw that small girl who is a girl like me but smallsmall and wow, it's making me think about SO many out there things. Like today I was thinking about what if there was a new color like not even like Purple or Pink that I believe in both but what if it was Grey-Red?? I know I know I CANNOT stop laughing at this like what a good joke how out there it is! Today at the beginning of Black (none) I closed my eyes and I did make believe that it was Grey-Red and it felt SO good and different and SO Grey-Red! My whole girl body self felt like I was made of all deersilk love of all things!!! WOW!!!

My friendfriend Buttz has a thing that he wants to show you, so I helped him write it (this is just me pretending make believe because Buttz is not a talker but this is a fun game for me and for Buttz that I pretend about). (I'm going to put him on the keyboard and let him write to you).

Jkdxfgtofvidsjknhjmkikutkjrrjktkr5tortfyhijo9i87yttrdtgfhg mjjhymmnye4ktujmhy3eikmjy fv n nbn r nre bn be3 dc tjjtrreer rerrerr re n n ne nd n n mjr ™, kyyytyyçtyt,t tr mgf nre de dde ewe we3nhrmt5mt6y6u7yu7jujyhmhnmjklkoopi9oo9oopoiiuujukop""""

OPujyyuttytr5eedewwqqwweqqwee3rweddssdaasQaaqQa sdasasdasasasds fn fcvvgbn nmm, ,m .,l;ooiuiyyghbnkmlkl;l;kl jk,trklr,k/fgfkfggg.j.ççüúyç¼çúçüyç6,küúçüúçüçüþgçgfvcgfgfk,g,k kkt55ttrfggtrfvg.kj,kk ki.oi8O

Anyway that was from Buttz who is a SOSWEET smallest friend of all! I hope you liked it! What a story!

Best love forever to my loveliest beautiful,
Muriel Claudia Edeltraud-Lilybridge

•°•

Dearestest DLMCE-L,

I THINK I HAVE FOUND A SECRET!!!!! Okay so right now it is Orange-White and I just had thirdmeal past secondsleep and do you remember how I said about during Black (none) I was closing my eyes and doing make-believe to see a made up color called Grey-Red?? I DID IT AGAIN and it wasn't even Black (none) anymore but now it's like every time I close my eyes it is Grey-Red, like without even trying it is Grey-Red!!!! How like a river glorious is this perfect peace!! That is a phrase I learned from my friend Christlike Reverence who is a friend with all kinds of fun words that I like a lot and don't always understand. Christlike Reverence has a LOT of a word that is God and it is always like that like God and she has words about how amazing God is for all kinds of reasons and stuff. There are a lot of things I think are amazing like I think my friends are amazing including my newest friend Annmarie Loudermilk who I haven't seen in awhile but is still amazing and I think Pets-colored is amazing and I think believing in Purple is amazing and I think that time I saw Pink (I KNOW I SAW PINK) was amazing and I think I am amazing and I think you are ESPECIALLY amazing and maybe all of those things together is God. Still lots of words I don't know which is okay because maybe after time I can figure out those like I figured out God!! Wow God is amazing!!

Love forever wow so much♪♪•√°→∆
Muriel Claudia

•°•

Hello hello beautiful next me!!!

Today I wanted to talk about my friends more. Elvis and Camshaft are very good friends of mine! They stay in my sleeping place on the sometimes when I am not asleeping, but mostly they are good in their home which is next to the sleepingplace on the bottom side of it and not the other side of it. One time I moved my sleepingplace to the middle of the room and oh my gosh it was so different and exciting for awhile! I got to be in a whole new place I had never been to with the sleepingplace in the middle of the room because the place where the sleepingplace was before did not have a single thing in it! Except for the things that had got under the sleeping place which were very interesting and sometimes smells came from there so it was a new smells place sort of like the other smells place I have. I don't really like going to smells places because there is too too much eyewater and what am I even doing with all of this eyewater???? But sometimes I need smells if I don't have enough eyewater around so that is good but also it can be hard to breathe if smells are too much smells.

ANYWAY I was saying that I have such good friends in Elvis and Camshaft! Elvis is pretty small but not as small as Buttz but pretty small!! He showed up a long time ago one day when it was Green I think. It was probably Green because I have had some friends show up when it was Green but it was all so so long ago how am I even supposed to remember????? I DON'T KNOW. Anyway, Elvis is not as softs as Salad-Bar or Marjorie With the Ears or some of my other friends so that is why they DO NOT live in the sleepingplace because I like it to be soft in my sleepingplace except sometimes when I do not take them out or I don't know just want to be REALLY silly and sleep next to a not so soft friend like Elvis or Christlike Reverence or another one. I DREW MORE PICTURES ALSO OF THEM. I want to eventually have pictures of ALL OF MY FRIENDS!!!!

•°•

Muriel Claudia Edeltraud-Lilybridge FROM THE DAYSLATER,

GOSH OKAY SO, where do I even start?? Okay okay, do you remember how I was talking about how I could find the Grey-Red when I closed my eyes like I did before in the last time I wrote to you, my dearest dayslater girl? WELL, okay so just a little bit ago I decided to explore the part of the room where it seems all of these small girls are coming from (first Annmarie Loudermilk, and then Another, which is the name I forgot to tell you but it's the name that I decided to call the version of me that is like me but so so smallsmall). I went into that corner and because it's a corner I don't look at much, there are some surprises there that aren't really surprises but like are things there that I don't look at much, like for example one of my friends who lives there, Cabin-boy, who I don't talk to as much but is still a wonderful friend for me to visit every sometimes, was hanging out and so it was very good to see Cabin-boy again. Also, there was some food that is now not-food because I didn't eat it while it was food still. It looked like some smallsmall had been eating it and I am guessing it was Annmarie Loudermilk but WHO KNOWS because apparently this is just a whole bunch of smallest eater girls over here now that I have found two. Anyway, so I was looking over there and I thought, huh, I wonder what this place looks like in Grey-Red, so I closed my eyes and sure enough, Grey-Red and my tummy did flipflips because I was looking at the verysame version of myself as a smallgirl that I saw before?? She was eating the not-food and playing with her feet, which I do sometimes too so I get it. I was afraid of having the feeling but I didn't have the feeling at all, just the flipflips, which are fine and totally okay because I know how to have flipflips. I said hi to her and she looked up at me!!! Then I got nervous and opened my eyes and no more Grey-Red then and she went away and came here to write this letter to you because it felt soso important to tell you even though I know you are dayslater and already know. I'm not sure why that is!

So, this is a thing that I found here and wow, it's so much of a thing that I found! I decided that she needed a name since apparently she was living here but in the Grey-Red version of here and so I named her Another, because I am me and she is like me but Another me. So she is named Another, which is such a good and perfect name! I hope she wants to be a friend and oh gosh what if she was a small talker girl? Like I am a big talker girl and so maybe small-me is a talker girl but just at a different size??? I so wish I could hear what you have to say about this because you know what happens!! Aaaaa I feel silly writing to you like this. It feels like why am I telling you all of these things you already know? Then I remember that I am the dayslaterself to my beforeself and when I go back and read those things I wrote to me now I mostly feel like oh my gosh my pastself is so beautiful and strong and good! I mostly want to comfort her and be happy with her and tell her about all the new exciting things that will happen and not to be so scared! Because a lot of times when I read my old writing I remember how I was feeling and that even sometimes when I write like I am happy I am actually secretscared also along with the happy. Not that the happy isn't real, just that it also has a secretscaredandlonely part to it that is always there always I guess.

Right now it is about to be Pets-colored and so I'm going to go because I want to cuddle up with friends and relax and spend time with Pets-colored because she is so beautiful and good. I love writing to you. You fulfill so much about me.

ALL THE LOVEST LOVE FOREVER TO YOU MY DEAREST DAYSLATER VERSION OF MURIEL CLAUDIA EDELTRAUD-LILYBRIDGE THE BESTEST GIRL IN THE WHOLE EVERYTHING ROOM,

Muriel Claudia Edeltraud-Lilybridge of the rightnow×¶ • ° • ¶¶× × Δ¶° ×°°

• ° •

MCE-L of the Latertime,

I am so sleeeepy right now. I am about to have lastsleep after my nice Pets-colored time. It was so good as always to see Pets-colored. I love her. Just for fun I went to Grey-Red after Pets-colored and saw Another for a little bit. I touched her small hand with my finger and she touched my finger with her smallhand! It was so perfect!! She IS a talker, which is absolutely the best thing I have ever ever ever heard ever?? She said to me a thing that I did not understand but I guess there are a bunch of things I do not understand which is okay but I do very very much want to understand this small Another girl. This is what she said but it was more like a song but this is what she said to me:

Zim zum, zim zum,
mahles mahles zim zum.
Zim zum, zim zum,
porpor porpor zim zum.

I was so surprised I jumped up and opened my eyes and fell over and ran and jumped into my sleepingplace again with my friends Salad-Bar and Marjorie With the Ears and Tremaine of the Antler and Elvis all around me to make me feel safe and I shook and shook and said the names of all my friends to myself over and over and over and eventually I got so sleepy like I am now. So I guess that is the story of that. So I just wanted to type this because I know it is all so very exciting even though I am almost asleep as I am writing this. Aaaa this is such a big deal I want to write so much more but I am sososo sleeepyyyy.

Aaaaaaa°ΔΔ • °Δ • • •

Goodnight my dayslatrrrrrrrrrrrrrr loveeeeeee

I love u forever ° • ×,
MCE-L from the rightnow

• ° •

Dear dear DLS,

It is now Yellow and I want to talk about small girls. Small girls are beautiful and I love them. They are girls, like me, but small. Also they sometimes are also not at all like me except that they are girls. A girl is a thing that is beautiful and wow, I guess a lot of things are

beautiful and so a lot of things are girls. Sometimes I don't think I
am beautiful but I am beautiful and I am a girl. When I was a small
girl I decided that I would be a girl when I got bigger because girls
are beautiful and I wanted to be beautiful. The bigbig secret is that
I was already beautiful back then but I DIDN'T EVEN KNOW
IT. Wowgosh.

The smallgirls I know are:

me when I was little

Annmarie Loudermilk

Another

Buttz.

If I could be small again I would try it because it would be fun
to be different than I am now for a little bit but I wouldn't want it
for always because I used to be small and I don't want to go back, I
want to go forward to be with you, Dayslater!

These are ten things I like about small girls:

How they are small

How they are beautiful

How they are girls of all the girls there are

How they are pretty (not the same as beautiful)

How they are hungry

How they discover secrets with their feet and in their hair

How they like themselves when they like themselves

How they are terrifying when they are terrifying

How they curl up into themselves with a pillow sometimes

How they drink water and know what it is to be warm

That's all I have to say about small girls right now. I love them
a lot. I wish that you could talk back to me.

I love you,
Muriel Claudia Edeltraud-Lilybridge

•º•

Dearest Pastself version of Muriel Claudia Edeltraud-Lilybridge,

I hope this isn't scary. I am the version of you from the later on and I have SO SO MANY THINGS TO TELL YOU. I know when I was you I wished so very much that I could say things to myself and talk back and forth like where I would say one thing and then I would say another thing but that the I who was saying it back was somehow different than the I that was saying it like where I had a talker friend who was also me! And here I am! Writing to you!× Δ¶° ×ºº

I think I can write to you as much as I want now and so I don't want to say a lot right now because I know this will be a lot a lot a lot and you will need to run away and lay with your friends for awhile after seeing this at all. So you should do that. But also. I want to say. PLEASE DO NOT TALK TO THE SMALL GIRL WHO IS CALLED ANOTHER. She was sent by The Feeling!!

But don't be scared. She can't hurt you either you just have to ignore her and be with your friends and talk to me and spend time with your Pets-colored and TAKE CARE OF YOUR OWN SELF, MURIEL CLAUDIA. GOSH I LOVE YOU. I KNOW THIS IS HARD. YOU CAN DO THIS. YOU WILL BE OKAY. •º¶××•º•ºº

Love so much SO MUCH SO SO MUCH FOREVER,
Muriel Claudia Edeltraud-Lilybridge of the Dayslater

Chapter Three

i dreamt someone wanted to hurt me
but no one can hurt me when i'm not even real

-Kristie Shoemaker, "i can be whatever you need"

Dear Muriel Claudia Edeltraud-Lilybridge of Latertimes,

Today when it was Red, I was beautiful. It was the most incredible feeling, being beautiful. I spent time being beautiful and while I was beautiful I sang wordless things. Things I half-remember from my smallness. My beautiful smallness. Red is a time for singing and being beautiful, I have decided. It is a time for these things. Yes.

It is now a good time to stop being beautiful and instead to write. I have had trouble figuring out what to write. I spent time being very excited and I spent time being very scared and I spent time being very tired and now I have spent time being beautiful. And singing, which I think will always make a person more beautiful. I'm not sure why I think that but it feels true.

The room feels smaller today, since I received your letter, dayslater self. I feel like I could touch opposite walls with my elbows. This isn't true, but it feels true. Maybe that is also the case with the singing.

On your advice I haven't approached the Grey-Red again, or Another. I don't know anything else to say about that. If you want to tell me more, that would be good. It is okay if you don't. I trust you, Muriel Claudia Edeltraud-Lilybridge. How can I not, with a name like that?! ×Δ°˜ •

I call myself that name too, as you well know. After I was beautiful I picked up my bed and saw grass underneath. In the grass were small rocks with markings on them. They didn't say anything important. I went to feed them to my friends as treats, but my friends weren't hungry.

I wonder what was here before my smallness. Have I always been here? Was I small forever until I wasn't? There are so many things I don't understand. I feel small smallsmall still in what I understand. Maybe you can help with this.

I am feeling very wispy now and so I am going to go lie in bed and wisp. Does this writing seem extra wispy to you? Lastsleep I had a dream. In it, a deer burst from my teeth, sweating orange tears of science and communication. There was also a very slippery hammer and 15 snails in small hats. Maybe later I will check the grass under my bed for snails. Maybe they need hats. Maybe that is what my dream was telling me. Maybe I am to be a hatmaker!

•°•

Dearest Muriel Claudia Edeltraud-Lilybridge from Beforetimes,

I want to teach you a word. The word is "sky." You've seen it before, though you won't remember it, because it was one of those words you never understood. No one ever taught you that word. You haven't had any context for it. Turn to page 312 in Christlike Reverence. Use the little numbers in the bottom corner. Look for 312. There should be a page, "Nearer, My God, to Thee". There are two lines there: "Or if, on joyful wing cleaving the sky, / sun, moon, and stars forgot, upward I fly."

Imagine there was no ceiling. Imagine instead that the air just went up and up. Now imagine no walls either. Imagine a room so big that you could walk forever and keep finding more. It sounds scary but it isn't. It is scary at first, but it isn't dangerous. It's the opposite. It is the most glorious thing, Muriel Claudia.

I can't wait to tell you about the sun.

<3

Lateryou

•°•

Dear most beautiful beautiful always my most lovely dayslater Muriel Claudia Edeltraud-Lilybridge,

I am not sure if I even know at all any of the things you are talking about but I found that page in Christlike Reverence and you are RIGHT it is just absolutely the verysame word that is the word that you said before in the thing you sent me on this screen!!!! I am so excited????? Pleaseplease if you know do tell me all about how you made the walls go away and then the ceiling go away and have there be more space than all of the space in the whole room and even more than that!!?? I can NOT even imagine what that is like but I want to be the sun or whatever too!!

UM, sorry if this is weird?? But um, could you tell me like... everything? What happened that you know about all of this and how dayslater are you?? It is Cherry-Red going to be White again soon and I reallyreally want to know just about every stuff that you have been up to?

•°•

Dearest deardear Muriel Claudia Edeltraud-Lilybridge,

After I wrote to you, I sat in my sleeping pile and brought my eyewater jar because it felt like I was going to make eyewater but I didn't. I just stared at the jar. It was Second Green and I could see the Second-Greeniness reflected in the little bit of eyewater left in it still from last time. I usually make eyewater at least once a day.

I felt a little bit sleepy and I think being in the sleeping place and feeling kind of hopeless made me into a big big sleepy girl. I said "I think I'm going to go to sleep now," and then I went to sleep.

I had a dream. In the dream I saw a room that was the biggest room I could imagine. It was like when I was thinking about how the room looks to Annmarie Loudermilk. How to such a smallgirl the floor and the room is soso big?? Or like how you were talking about sky. What a sky is. Where there were no walls or ceiling. This was like that. Up above it was all Orange-White with blotches. On the bottom it was all pinkpinkpink! It was so good to see Pink! It was real Pink like PinkPink???? But I am saving the best part. I can't believe what the best part was????

I know you know already but I still need to need to tell you. The blotches up high?? Were PURPLE??????!!!!!!!!!!

I don't remember most of the dream. I know there was more. I want to sleep again reallyreallysoon. I think there is a lot more for us. We have so much of a place out there in my dream. It's all in there. All of it.

Sleep well forever I love you so much,

Muriel-Claudia

•ᵒ•

Dear Dayslater of Someone Who I Guess Is My Self But I Don't Know Because I Thought I Would Be Nicer to My Own Very Self,

I don't know why you're not responding. It has been too too long and you have not said anyword at ALL. I don't know what you think you're doing, or if you got distracted like sometimes how I will think of something but then get distracted doing another thing and then forget about doing the thing I was going to do because I'm playing with Marjorie With the Ears and touching her ears on my cheeks because they're so so soft. I feel like you should have responded. I asked you a question, which was to tell me everything and you did not tell me everything. In fact you have told me nothing. Not any one thing. Not a word. Please please pleaseplease tell me 1 word but really like more than one word because if you just sent me one word I would still be kind of mad at you because if you CANNOT tell I am mad at you right now. At me who is you. UGH.

I think you should be nicer to me, because I will become you.

Anyway, today I guess I will tell you what happened today because I guess I will. Today I saw sky. It was really beautiful. It was actually the most beautiful thing I have ever seen and I have seen beautiful things before like snails or like Camshaft. This was different though. It was big.

The room right now is like a whole different place because there is now sky everywhere around it. It is kind of scary like you said but also it is bigbigbig in a way that is exciting. I don't know what to do with all this space. I see like there are other things I haven't seen before, like big things I haven't seen before that are now in the room with me except it's bigger than it was and I don't know if this is even still the room even though it is definitely the room because my things are here. I could probably go to see the bigger things but they seem far. I will probably stay here with my things. PLEASE WRITE BACK TO ME AND TELL ME EVERYTHING PLEASE.

I miss you.

Love,

Muriel Claudia Edeltraud-Lilybridge the girl who is daysbefore to you and who is you and who is mad at you and wants you to write everything to her please now do it please.

•°•

Dear Muriel Claudia Edeltraud-Lilybridge,

I want to tell you something and this thing is very important. I told you that I am you from the dayslater. This is true but in the dayslater you become something very different than you are now. It turns out that you are made of dreams, the daughter of a god of dreams. You have heard of God from Christlike Reverence and even though Christlike Reverence is very confused about a lot of things you totally figured out what God is. What anygod is. I'm so proud of us for that. Anway, this means you will live a very long time and look many different ways. Right now I look like a bear that looks like something that you will eventually learn is called a mountain. Imagine if you put everything in your room in a pile, how big that pile would be. Now imagine that is bigger than anything you could imagine. Now imagine it's bigger still. That's me (you) right now. I know, it's weird but you will get used to it. The thing you find out when you live a very long time is that everything is weird and you get used to it. Except the ways that things get hurt. I will never get used to that.

I'm getting off track, though. There is someone I want you to meet. To do this you will need to fall asleep. When you fall asleep, I want you to dream a specific thing. It might take you some tries to do this but I know you can do it, because I am you from the dayslater and I did it. This is what I want you to dream:

There is a flat place that goes out as far as you can see in every direction. It's like the floor but no walls and nothing in the room.

This might take a few tries to figure out how to picture it but I think you can do it. Once you can do that, this is the really hard part. I want you to picture in the middle of the field is your room. The walls are Black (none). The walls are not on all sides of you. You are outside the room. It will look like a black cube.

I want you to climb one of the walls until you are on top of the black cube. On top of the ceiling of the room. There you will find a furry creature. It will be soft and covered in fur like your friends except the fur is more like the hair on your head but shorter like the time you pulled a bunch out and it came back smallsmall that tickled when you touched it.

The creature will come up to you and say something. It will talk to you. You might start to have the Feeling but I want you to keep going.

When the creature speaks it will say this:

"Hello, this is Binah, child of the Snows speaking, and you have reached the black cube. I'm not at cube right now, but if you'd like to leave a message, you can do so after the beep."

Then there will be a beep-sound. What comes after the beep is the rest of your life, and it will be long, and beautiful, and sad, and more full than you could ever imagine.

Thanks to Dogtail, Lily, Mara, Irene, Ramona and anyone else who read early versions of this. Without having y'all to talk to about this project I don't know where it would have ended up. Thanks to Ben for being stoked on publishing Rainbear!!!!!!!!! and being great to work with. Thanks to Jaime for helping me come up with the name "Rainbear". Thanks to Carrie and Frog and the Trans Lit Shit discord for listening to me as I tried to figure out what to do with this weird book. Thanks to Carly <3. Thanks to Shrek crew and queer Torah study crew and all my wonderful Oly weirdos. Thanks to Xava and Michael for having me on your podcast. Thanks to everyone who's reading and has read and supported my work over the years. You're all incredible and it means a lot to me to be able to share this with you all.

Never Angeline Nørth is author of the books *Sea-Witch* (Inside the Castle, 2020), *Careful Mountain* (CCM, 2016), *Sara or the Existence of Fire* (Horse Less Press, 2014) and *Wolf Doctors* (Artifice Books, 2014). She lives in beautiful Olympia, WA with her girlfriend, her girlfriend's boyfriend, their dog, a snake and two rats. She is online at never.horse.